The Talisman

The Talisman - Book VIII

The Talisman

Michael Harling

iv

Lindenwald LP Press

To Mitch and Charlie
Without whom there would be no story.

Also by Michael Harling

The Postcards Trilogy
Postcards From Across the Pond
More Postcards From Across the Pond
Postcards From Ireland

The Talisman Series
The Magic Cloak
The Roman Villa
The Sacred Tor
The Bard of Tilbury
The Crystal Palace
The White Feather
The Isle of Avalon

Finding Rachel Davenport

Chapter 1
Saturday, 4th of July 2020

Mitch

The Spitfire juddered as bullets slammed into the fuselage. I pushed the stick forward, diving and rolling to avoid the Messerschmitt. Bullets whizzed by on my left. Holes appeared in the wing, but the little Spitfire still responded. It was a tenacious plane, a miracle machine, really. I pulled back and went into a climb, trying to loop over the Messerschmitt, but the German stayed right behind me. Ahead now were the green fields of southern England, behind was the Messerschmitt and the grey, choppy waters of the Channel.

I did a barrel roll and pointed the plane straight down, gaining speed, zigging and zagging, desperately trying to shake off the German. But the bullets continued to fly around me, and the plane continued to jerk and sputter.

There was no one around to help. In the distance, I could see the rest of the squadron continuing their attack on the German bombers. I was alone, in a wounded Spitfire, screaming towards the icy water. I pulled back on the stick, struggling to level out and lose some of the speed I had used to outrun the Messerschmitt. I rolled the plane again, to the right, then left, and another round of bullets zipped past me. Smoke began to trail out of the engine, obscuring my view. I checked the instruments to be sure I was flying level. I wasn't. I gave it more power and pulled back on the stick but, try as I might, the Spitfire continued its downward plunge. Through the smoke, I glimpsed the grey water. There was no hope. The Messerschmitt had broken off, returning to the fight, already counting me as a kill.

I cut the throttle, pulled the stick. The plane moved closer to level, but it was no use trying to gain altitude. Through the haze of smoke, I saw the Channel getting closer, then I saw flames shooting from the plane's engine. It was now a toss-up if I would burn to death or drown.

The flames grew. Red and orange obscured my view. The plane hit the water, the windshield cracked and—

"Mitch!" It was Charlie, calling from the top of the stairway. "Mom wants to speak to you."

I sighed and set the joystick aside. It was no use saving the scenario, so I hit the ESC key and returned to the flight simulator's main screen. "Just me?"

Charlie came into my room. "No, both of us."

My insides grew cold. "You don't think—"

He shook his head. "No. I mean, I don't know. All I know is, she's sitting at the dining table with a package of some sort."

"But Granddad wouldn't have, couldn't have, sent us another gift."

"It won't matter if he did," Charlie said, already turning around, "the cloak is gone, so even if we're called, we can't go."

I thought about what that might mean. After our last adventure, we'd been so certain it had been our last that we gave the cloak to Mom so she could burn it. Dad just sort of forgot about the whole thing and life went back to normal and, when summer came this year, Mom didn't get crazy, and we didn't try to think up a way to get Granddad's gift before she did because we knew there wouldn't be one. We had been, in as much as it is possible, a happy family. And Charlie and I were glad to not be going on any more adventures.

It was the day of the full moon, Saturday, the 4th of July and, as far as I knew, no mysterious gifts had arrived. We'd been so caught up in preparing for the Independence Day celebrations that we hadn't even thought about it. We'd dressed in our cadet uniforms and marched with our troop in the parade down Wynantskill's main street. There had been speeches, a reading of *In Flanders Fields*, and a few mostly-on-key performances by the school band at the war memorial. After that, we'd broken up to prepare for the village barbecue.

Then Mom said she wanted us to go home and change even though no one else was. We asked why and she said she didn't want our new uniforms getting grass stains and barbecue sauce all over them. I thought that was a lame answer. I figured she just wanted to go home to rest. She'd been quiet and subdued all morning and I thought she might be coming down with a summer cold. Why she wanted us to go home with her, though, I couldn't guess. But Dad said it was a good idea, so she took us home in the car and we changed into our regular clothes and then waited because she said she had something to do. So, Charlie sat downstairs reading, and I played a quick game on my flight simulator. I was currently

3

running a WWII scenario, flying the Spitfire, and I wasn't doing so well, which was why I wanted to practice.

I got a flight simulator program two years earlier, after an adventure where I ended up flying a BE2c night fighter in a zeppelin raid. Despite the danger, I found I loved flying and, after the adventure, since I couldn't get a real airplane, I got the flight simulator game. I started out, naturally, with the BE2c, but soon grew tired of that. Then I found an add-on that included more modern planes, including the Spitfire. I really enjoyed flying that simulation and, even though I kept getting shot down, I was having a good time.

But now we had been summoned, and it didn't sound good.

◆

We found Mom sitting at the dining room table with a padded envelope in front of her. My heart dropped. It had to be another gift from Granddad, but Mom didn't seem angry. She just sat, with her elbows on the table and her head in her hands, staring at the tabletop.

The yearly ritual—the gift we got from Granddad and used, along with the magic cloak, to take us on what we called an adventure (but which was really a terrifying ordeal in some past era where there was constant danger and no indoor plumbing)—had come to an end. We were sure of that. Our last adventure was just that, our last one, so I wasn't sure what to think. We'd been certain there would be no more gifts. And even if there was, we couldn't go because we didn't have the cloak. It had been destroyed in the battle of Camlann and we'd only been able to return home by using Arthur's cloak. And we'd handed that over to Mom.

What if Granddad did send us another gift? What if we were expected to go on yet another adventure and we didn't have the cloak? Was that why Mom wasn't upset, because she knew we couldn't go anyway?

If Mom really did know about the cloak, and if so, how much, was something Charlie and I had discussed but never agreed on. She must have known something about the gifts and the cloak and the adventures, but we couldn't figure out how. Our last adventure had shown both Mom and Dad what the cloak could do, but we'd never talked about it. We'd just given up the cloak and no one said a word and we'd gone about our lives, happy that it was all behind us.

"I have something to tell you," Mom said, as we sat down at the table. She lifted her head and laid her hands on the envelope. I could see by the labels and the handwriting that it was from Granddad, and my insides did another flip. A gift? How, and why, and what good would it do without the cloak?

I expected Mom to launch into a lecture, but instead, she just started talking, as if she was relating some nostalgic story.

"Back at the turn of the century," she said, staring once again at the table, "when your father and I were newly married, and Mitch was not yet two months old, we went to a family gathering, a party, for one of your father's distant relatives, in Canada. She was turning 100 that year, on the first of October."

I felt the blood drain from my face. I did some

quick calculations. The first of October 2000 would be the 100th birthday of—

"Annie," I said. "You met Annie McAllister?"

Mom nodded.

I looked at Charlie. His face was as white as mine felt.

"She was a nice, old lady," Mom continued, "surprisingly chipper for someone her age. I felt a little out of my depth. The party was at the home of one of her relatives. I remember milling around, holding you," Mom glanced up in my direction, "and looking desperately for your father. I was alone in a room full of strangers. They were mostly strangers to your father too, but he was related to them. I was an outsider.

"Then this old woman came up to me. I didn't realize, at first, that it was Annie. There were several older women there. I figured it was one of them, but the woman introduced herself and I remember being amazed at how coherent she seemed, you know, for being a hundred. She said she had something to tell me.

"She led me outside, to a quiet corner of the patio, where we sat in over-sized, wicker chairs. I remember that someone brought us lemonade, which I was grateful for. It was hot, an Indian Summer, and the crush of people made it uncomfortably warm in the house, so I was glad to be away from them. I had to juggle Mitch on one arm while I sipped the drink, and I had no place to put it until Annie pulled a plastic patio table over. I felt a little uncomfortable, sitting with a stranger, and I was thinking I needed to find someplace to go and feed Mitch. Then this woman, this ancient woman who I had never met before, started telling me the most amazing things.

"She said there was a family story, passed down from mother to daughter, going back centuries. And now that I was part of the family, I needed to hear it. She spoke of a gap. Something about your father's great-great-grandfather. He came to America with his son and wife, but then his wife died, so when his son got married, there was no one to tell his bride the story, so the tale died out, and Annie needed to revive it by telling it to me.

"I remember being a little bored at this point. I didn't know much about your father's family. I think she told me she was a cousin, three or four times removed, or something like that."

I didn't need to do any calculations. I knew exactly where Annie sat in the family tree. She was my third cousin, four times removed. I stared at Mom, still not believing she had been told our story.

"By now, I was thinking I needed to get away from this woman," Mom said. "Not just because she was boring me, but I was starting to leak, and I needed to feed you."

"Mom," I said, "seriously, can't we skip that part?"

"I stopped being bored when she told me the rest," Mom said, staring at the tabletop. She seemed oblivious to us, caught up in her recollection. "I became alarmed, instead. She told me of visitors, two brothers, with red hair, the same age but not twins, who appeared to the family throughout the ages. These boys—knights, she called them—continue to visit. They come, she told me, when the Land is in peril, and I was to be ready for them. I would know them because they travelled with a cloak. A dark blue cloak."

She stopped then, shaking her head slightly. "I thought she was just spinning yarns," she said, her voice barely a whisper, "but then she said she had met them." She lifted her head and looked directly at me. "Did you?"

I opened my mouth but couldn't speak. I couldn't believe it. She had kept her promise, the promise she had made all the way back in—

"Nineteen-sixteen," Charlie said. "She was living in Horsham, with her cousin Maggie."

Mom blanched. "She gave you that feather," she said.

I still couldn't speak, so I just nodded.

"I thought … I thought she was a crazy old lady, and I was looking for a way to get away from her. Then she reached out to me, to you, and I started to panic. I knew she was crazy, but I didn't know if she was dangerous. I tried to sink into my chair. Then you turned to her, and smiled and grabbed her finger in your little fist and the two of you looked at each other and I thought I was going to faint.

"Then the woman, Annie, pulled her hand away. She smiled at me. She looked peaceful, content. I didn't know what to say, I was so confused. Then she stood up and said, 'Thank you.' And as she walked away, she told me there was a quiet bedroom upstairs in the house where I could feed Mitch. I was halfway there before I realized I had never told her Mitch's name."

"Someone could have told her," I said, finally finding my voice.

"Yes," Mom said, "but I didn't get that impression. She seemed to know you. It was really upsetting. When I finished feeding you, I sat in the room until your father came to find me. I was still confused and frightened, but I didn't tell him anything. I just said I wasn't feeling well. We left shortly after that. I never saw Annie, or any of the other relatives, again. I put the episode behind me and forgot all about it. Then your grandfather sent you that cloak."

"So, you knew all along?" Charlie asked.

"No," Mom said, "not really. I mean, how could anyone believe anything so ridiculous? I thought it was a coincidence, or a joke. Your Grandfather may have heard the story. Maybe he thought it was funny, or he wanted you to develop an interest in your family history. I didn't know. But I was certain it wasn't something that would transport you back in time.

"But the gifts kept coming. And each time they arrived—the quills, the play money, the shields, the glass cutters—you always went for the cloak, even though you ignored it for the rest of the year. And you changed. In the days after the gifts arrived, you'd be distant, quiet, and serious, like you'd grown older. I still couldn't believe you were the boys that old woman talked about. But I began to wonder, and I decided, if I could just keep your grandfather's gifts away from you, it wouldn't matter if it was real or not. Then, last year, the swords came, and you were so … you disobeyed us, you stole them, locked yourselves in your room and you … you disappeared. That was when I knew, really knew, it was all true."

She stopped talking then and covered her face with her hands. Charlie and I sat in awkward silence until she dug in her pocket for a tissue, wiped her eyes and continued.

"But, in a strange way, that made me feel better. I

9

wasn't crazy, it was really happening and, it was … over." She held the tissue to her nose and gazed at the tabletop again, staring at the envelope.

"Except it's not," I said, "is it?"

She shook her head, still holding the tissue to her face. With her free hand, she lifted one end of the envelope. A black disk, about the size of a hockey puck, clanked onto the table, followed by a sheet of paper covered in Granddad's scrawl.

My breath stopped. My stomach went cold.

It was the Talisman.

Chapter 2

Charlie

We stared at it for a few moments, Mom still sniffling, Mitch, his face white and his eyes wide, and me, with a lump of ice sinking down my chest and into my stomach. When no one made a move, I picked up Granddad's letter.

"Hell-o boys," It began. "I hope all is well." I skipped over the niceties, scanning for the important part. When I found it, I began reading out loud:

"I took a walk to see that old man in his what-not shop a few weeks back, the place where I find your gifts. It was gone. The whole building bulldozed under and everything around it chewed up. They say they're building a housing estate. I was, as they say here, gobsmacked. I was sure I wouldn't find anything to send you this year, but then I went to a car boot sale—that's a type of flea market where they have their stuff in the trunks of their cars instead of on folding tables. Anyway, there was a guy selling odds and ends and he had this strange stone and I felt compelled to buy it. I gave him a fiver for it. He wanted more, but I told him it was so beat up it wasn't worth …"

I laid the letter down.

The Talisman, if it was indeed the Talisman, looked scuffed up. It had lost its lustre, and there was a chunk chipped off one edge.

"I was going to throw it away," Mom said. "When it came this morning. I was ready to put it in the garbage, but then I opened it and that black thing fell into my hands, and …" Her voice cracked. She wiped her eyes and blew her nose and continued. "I hid it, instead. We were leaving, anyway, and I had no time, so I went and saw you march and heard the speeches and thought of all those brave boys who went to war, not because they wanted to, not because their mother's wished them to, but because they had a duty. It was smarmy, I know, but the feeling overcame me, and I knew I had to give you the choice."

I looked at her, suddenly afraid. "What choice?"

She looked at me with sad eyes. "Pick up the stone," she said.

I reached out and took the Talisman in my hands. Its surface no longer looked like a mirror, but it still held my gaze, and soon I was drawn in, slipping through the black hole into a world beyond. And in the blackness, I saw fire. Flames danced around me, but I wasn't afraid, not of the fire. I felt joy, a heart bursting joy that made me want to laugh out loud. But there was something else. The memory of a sharp crack so loud it stung my ears. A searing pain in my chest made me gasp. I wanted to cry, to shout, to scream. Yet the joy remained, even as I felt helpless, terrified, alone, and enraged. The two emotions were ripping me apart. I dropped the Talisman and blinked, surprised to find myself back in the dining room. Sweat trickled down my forehead into my eyes. I wiped it away.

"What did you see?" Mom asked.

I took a breath. "It's not what I saw, it's what I felt." I picked up the Talisman and ran my hand over its scarred surface. I was no longer afraid of it. It had shown me what I needed to see, what I needed to do. But there would be a cost. Something goes wrong. Horribly wrong. I pushed the feeling, and the Talisman, aside. Thinking about it wouldn't help. And besides, we weren't going anywhere. I felt guilty and glad at the same time.

I laid the Talisman down and Mom slid it across the table to Mitch, as if it was a token in some bizarre board game.

"And you?"

Mitch, his face still white, said nothing. He picked up the Talisman and peered into it. Slowly, his colour returned, and his breathing became even. He stared into the Talisman for another few seconds, then calmly put it down. "Water," he said.

Mom looked at us with such sadness it made me want to cry. Then I realized something that made my insides go even colder. "You touched the Talisman. It showed you something."

She looked down and nodded.

"What did you see?" Mitch asked.

Mom covered her face with her hands. "It was horrible. I can't ..." I thought she was going to start crying again, but she took a breath and laid her hands on the table, next to the Talisman. "It was like a movie, but also like I was really there, high up, watching. There was a city. London, I think, because I saw Big Ben, standing in the rubble. There were people, lying dead in the streets, and tanks and soldiers everywhere. German soldiers, with guns."

She started shuddering then and drew another

breath.

"The people in that city, they were crying, screaming in terror, and that's when I dropped it. But, even as I did, I heard a voice. Clear, so clear I couldn't believe the rest of you didn't hear it."

All the times I had looked into the Talisman, it had never spoken to me. "What did it say?"

"It said, 'The Land is in peril.'"

We sat silent, shocked. Then Mitch said, "The Germans must have won the war."

"They won because the Talisman wasn't in its place in the Sacred Tor," I said. "And we can't go back to fix it." I looked at Mitch, and then at Mom. "What is this going to mean? We're supposed to go back, to put things right. But we can't do that now."

Mom said nothing. She stood and went to the hall closet and pulled out an old raincoat. A bulky, battered thing I had seen hundreds of times, hanging in the dark. She laid it on the table and opened it up. Inside was a blanket. She pulled the blanket out and spread it over the tabletop.

It wasn't a blanket. It was the cloak.

Chapter 3

Mitch

"But you burned it," Charlie said.

I ran my hand over the fabric. It was clean and, incredibly, repaired. "You said you destroyed it, last year when we gave it to you."

"I was going to," Mom said. "I had every intention, and every reason to. By then, I knew that woman, Annie, wasn't lying, or telling fables. It was real, and all the things she'd told me that I didn't want to know came back to me and I knew I had to protect you, I had to destroy the cloak, but I couldn't. I just hid it away. I worked on it when no one else was around. In a strange way, it brought me comfort. Until today."

She touched the cloak, stroking it lightly with her fingertips. "I couldn't have you going, not this time. I was determined to protect you. But then that vision, that horrific vision, and the words, the speeches, the old men with their medals. They hadn't wanted to go. They didn't see themselves as heroes. They were just doing what they had to do. But for a mother to send her boys into that, knowing … No mother should have to make that choice. So, I'm not making it. It's your choice. The cloak is here. You have your grandfather's rock. It's your choice … your choice."

Her voice cracked again, and we looked away.

"There's not really a choice," I said to Charlie, my heart already pounding.

Charlie nodded. "We have to."

"Maybe it won't end so badly," I said.

He shrugged. "We know what we have to do. Nothing else matters."

Mom started balling at that, so we stopped talking and went and hugged her. I thought she was going to break my ribs when she hugged me back.

"How are we going to do this?" Charlie asked, his voice muffled against Mom's shirt. "I'm not exactly ready to drift off to sleep right now."

Mom let go, wiping her eyes and sniffing. "I have a plan."

She led us into the spare room, where she had been since we arrived home. Our cadet uniforms were there, with all the insignia removed.

"Put these on," she said, and left the room.

We did as we were told, but neither of us knew why.

"I think maybe Annie told Mom more than she is letting on," Charlie said.

"Do you think we should ask her?"

Charlie tucked in his shirt and tightened his belt. "Would it make a difference?"

I finished buttoning my shirt. I didn't bother to answer; Charlie was right, there was no use asking and no good would come from us knowing any more than we already did.

When we were ready, we found Mom upstairs, in my bedroom, holding the cloak. "You look like little soldiers," she said when she saw us. Then she started crying again.

"We're not that little," Charlie said. "We're

nineteen."

Then she cried some more.

We sat on the bed and waited. She gave us the Talisman and Charlie put it in his pocket.

"Take these," she said, handing us each a pill.

I looked at mine. "What are these? Sleeping pills?"

Mom offered us a bottle of water. "I saved a few," she said, looking at the floor, "from when I was … when I wasn't feeling well. These are the last of them."

We swallowed the pills. Two years ago, we had split one in half and that had been enough to put us to sleep. These were going to knock us out.

She had us lie side by side, then covered us with the cloak, all but our heads. I relaxed and tried to let the pill do its work, but Mom kept looking down at us with tears dripping from her eyes. When I became sleepy, she kissed me on the forehead. Then she kissed Charlie, who already seemed to be sleeping, and pulled the cloak over our heads.

"Good-bye," she said.

Then everything went black.

Chapter 4
Friday, 9 August 1940

Charlie

"Hey, numbskulls! You're in the wrong bunk."

I tried to open my eyes, but they felt glued shut. "Wha …?"

A hand shoved my shoulder and sudden light stung my eyes as the cloak was whipped away.

"How did you blokes get in here? I was waiting for you at the gate."

Mitch stirred beside me. "Where are we?"

I rubbed my eyes and turned my head as far as I could. We were in a long, low building, roughly made, with exposed beams and naked light bulbs hanging from the peaked ceiling. There were other beds besides the one we were in, but they weren't lined up like in a barracks, they were spaced around the cavernous building, each in its own room—or what would be a room if there had been walls. There were trunks, bedside tables, lamps, cabinets, and dressers. On the walls, coats and hats, with military insignia, hung from hooks. It looked like a World War Two prison camp from those old movies, complete with photos of young women pinned up near the beds.

There were few windows, and I noticed the wall closest to us was made of stone. Everything else was wooden. Except for the guy standing over us, holding our cloak. He was young and slender, with close-cropped red hair, wearing a blue uniform with a winged insignia on it. And he was glaring down at us.

"One eight eight Squadron, RAF Horsham," he said, "where do you think? And this embarrassment is the Officers' Quarters. Now get out of that bunk before Bugs comes back and finds you."

I yawned and climbed out of the bed and stood in front of him.

"What sort of uniforms are those?" he asked. "And where's your gear?" He held out the cloak. "And what's this?"

I looked at the cloak, and then at our inquisitor, who seemed to be about my age. "You sure ask a lot of questions."

He grinned and I felt a wave of relief. "Not as many as the CO is going to ask, and he won't be as polite about it. And the first thing he's going to want to know is how the hell you got in here."

Mitch got off the bed and stood next to me. "Who are you? If you don't mind my asking."

"I'm the officer you were supposed to be turned over to. So, I ask again, how did you get here?"

"Do you mean in here," Mitch asked, "or how did we get to the base?"

"Both. And which one of you is Pilot Officer Johnathan Kent?"

Mitch and I looked at each other. "I am," Mitch said, half a second before I was going to.

The officer turned to me. "Then you must be Pilot Officer Richard Hamlin."

"So, I must," I said, "and you?"

He tossed our cloak on the bed and placed his fists on his hips. "Flight Lieutenant James Wyman," he said, pronouncing lieutenant as LEFT-tenant.

Mitch snapped to attention and saluted. "Sir!" he said. I did the same.

James returned a half-hearted salute. "At ease. Now, once more, where is your gear and how did you get here?"

"Well," I said, trying to line my thoughts up, "we got a ride."

"From where?"

"It's a little confusing," Mitch said. "You know how it is. Go there, wait here, put that over there. Someone told us to get in a jeep and—"

"A jeep? Is that one of your Canadian colloquialisms."

"A small, general-purpose military vehicle," I said, hoping to confuse things further.

"Army, or RAF"

I looked at Mitch. "Well …"

"Army," Mitch said.

James shook his head and looked at the floor. "Figures. What did they do, drop you off at the first gate they came to?"

I wasn't sure if it was a trap, but there was nowhere else to go. "Well, yeah."

"They were supposed to deliver you to me at the Main Gate."

"I suppose," I said, "but we just—"

"And you gear?"

"They said it would be delivered presently," Mitch said.

"You're telling me the Army just dropped you off without following established protocol, and managed to lose your gear in the process, and then you just wandered into an RAF Base without anyone challenging you?"

"Yes," Mitch said, then added, "sir."

James started pacing, still shaking his head. "Typical. They were probably afraid they'd get their asses handed to them for not having your gear. But even if you were dropped off at the Upper Gate by a military vehicle, the guards should have challenged you."

"Yes, sir," Mitch said, "they should have."

James stopped pacing and folded his arms across his chest. "Well, they'll hear about it. But first, I need to get you to Captain Follow Me—" He stopped abruptly. "I mean, Wing Commander Farrow, and he won't want to hear about this balls-up, so listen: You were delivered to me at the Main Gate. You were sent on ahead of your gear. It will be arriving soon. Do not volunteer any information, especially about the army having dropped you off."

"Yessir!" we said in unison.

James looked at us, his arms still folded tight across his chest. "Commander Farrow is going to have kittens if he sees you like this. No proper uniforms, no gear, just a blanket. And if you got separated from your gear, where did you get that from?"

"It's a keepsake," I said. "We always keep it with us."

"We?"

I felt myself go red. "Well, it really belongs to …" I thought hard, trying to remember who Mitch was supposed to be. "… Kent, but I've sort of adopted it since we've been travelling together."

"Well, it won't last five minutes in here if you leave it laying around. You'll be assigned a bed and a locker eventually, but you'd better let me put that in mine for the time being."

I gave him the cloak. He went to a nearby bed that had a cabinet, like a portable closet, standing against the wall near it. He tossed the cloak inside, shut and locked it. Then he turned to us. "Come with me. You'll need to check in with Squadron Leader Fulbright, first, then Flight Commander Farrow wants to see you, so I'll make the introductions, and try to keep things smooth."

As he led us from the barracks, other men came in, all dressed in the same blue uniform as James.

"Red, you jammy bastard," one of them said, punching James in the arm as he walked by. "Old Follow-Me gave us his most boring lecture yet. Where were you?"

"Special Assignment," James said.

"What? Babysitting the Canucks?" the man looked at us. "These are the Canucks, right?"

James introduced us around, to people with names like Chalky, Yo-Yo, Ditter, Zero and Bugs, whose bed, I assumed, we had appeared in. They were gruff but friendly, squeezing my hand painfully and giving us the ritual back-slaps.

When we got away from them, we stepped outside. The first thing I saw was a fence, over ten feet tall, made of upright poles and barbed wire. It wasn't far away, and it ran straight along an unpaved road. Across the road was the farmhouse we had stayed in when we had visited in 1916. I looked back at the barracks and realized it was on the site of the house we had appeared in, and that the parts of the house that had remained standing after the fire had been incorporated into the new structure, which

22

appeared to have been a barn.

All around, where there used to be fields, were wooden buildings, strange, semi-cylindrical structures roofed in corrugated metal that I later learned were called Nissen huts, rutted dirt tracks, vehicles, and men in military uniforms, some blue, others khaki. A British flag flew from a pole atop a crude, wooden tower and, beyond that, the ground levelled off. There were no tracks, just a flat field of short grass.

And on the far side of the field were about a dozen airplanes.

Chapter 5

Mitch

"Spitfires," I said.

James followed my gaze to a neat row of single-engine airplanes, angled propeller-out, along the far edge of the field. Even in the dull light, they seemed to glow, and brought to mind green dragon flies. They stood ready, almost eager, to roll along the packed earth and buzz into the sky.

"They are beauties, eh?" James said. "How do they compare to the Spits you flew in Canada?"

"I've never flown a Spitfire."

James turned to me, his brow furrowed. "I thought you were pilots."

"I, um, we … I have flown," I said, "I am a pilot. I just haven't flown a Spitfire."

"What have you flown?"

"Well, other aircraft," I said, trying to sound like I knew what I was talking about. "I learned on a BE2c, but I've flown a Curtiss P-36 Hawk and a P-51 Mustang." Which were two of the planes from my flight simulator.

"What's a P-51?" James asked.

"It's just, you know, a plane. A fighter."

"But no Spitfire?"

I've logged a lot of hours on the simulator with the Spitfire."

"Simulator?" James held his head in his hands for a few seconds, then glared at Charlie. "What about you?"

"Sure," Charlie said, smiling, "I've flown lots of Spitfires. Great plane. Nothing like it."

James eyed him suspiciously. "This isn't going to go down well." He paced a small circle, his hands behind his back, staring at the ground. "Look," he said, "this is turning into a dog's breakfast. First, you leave me standing at the gate, and now you don't seem to know what an airplane does. I don't know what the Canucks are playing at, sending a couple of yokels over here, but Fulbright isn't going to stop with just chewing you two out. This is going to reflect badly on me, and I'm taking that personally."

He stopped and stared at us. We stood to attention for a few seconds, saying nothing.

"James," I said, "we—"

"That's Flight LEFT-tenant Wyman, to you."

"Flight Left-tenant Wyman," I said, keeping my eyes forward and my back straight, "we are pilots. I have a lot of flight experience. We just don't have the same equipment over there that you have here. I am confident I can fly the Spitfire, given the chance."

"The chance? The chance?" James said, his voice rising. Several of the men in khaki, who were digging a drainage ditch along the side of the gravel road, looked our way.

James sighed. "Fulbright is going to have kittens when he hears this. And Farrow … God help us. Listen, I'll do most of the talking." He looked at Charlie. "And you, just keep your mouth shut. And try to look like a proper airman."

He marched us down a wide lane of hard-pack

25

earth covered in gravel, past wooden buildings whose timber had not yet weathered, and rows of gleaming Nissan huts. Some had wooden planks with hand-painted letters in front of them reading things like "Officers' Mess," "NCO Club" and "Security."

"They've knocked this base up sharpish," James said when he saw me looking. "We needed it in a hurry, so it's not quite as salubrious as the conditions you enjoyed back in Canada, especially the pilots' quarters."

I nodded as if I understood. "It's fine, really."

James chuckled. "Certainly, if you like living like an enlisted man. Don't fret, they've promised us proper officers' quarters as soon as they kit out the rest of the base. Seems we pilots are on the bottom rung."

"We've slept in barns before," I told him. "It's fine by us."

"Yes, but … how did you know it used to be a barn?"

"Farmhouse across the road," I said. "What else would it have been."

He rubbed his chin. "Hmmm, quite."

We turned down a gravel path that led to a Nissan hut with a sign reading, "Squadron Leader.". James knocked on the door, which was opened almost immediately by a young man wearing round glasses and a military uniform.

"Flight Lieutenant Wyman to see Squadron Leader Fulbright," James said.

The young man pushed his glasses back up his nose and pointed at us. "And they are?"

"New pilots."

He disappeared inside, leaving the door open for us.

It was a small office, with a few wooden file cabinets, small tables, some chairs, and a desk, behind which sat a burly man with a crew cut and a rugged face. He wore a blue uniform, like James, but with more stripes. An RAF cap sat on the edge of the desk, leaning against a strange black device I took to be a telephone.

James walked to the desk with us behind him. He stood to attention and saluted, so we did too.

"The new pilots, sir, from Canada."

Fulbright returned a quick salute but didn't stop marking the chart he was looking at.

"As if I don't have enough problems, you bring me rookie pilots."

James continued to stare straight ahead.

"Yes, sir."

Fulbright sighed. "Give me your flight logs."

I looked at Charlie, rolled my eyes, and then turned to Fulbright. "We don't have them. Sir."

Fulbright laid his pencil down and looked up. When he spoke, his voice was quiet and contained, which made it even more menacing. "You don't have them?"

"No, sir."

"And where are they?"

"With our gear. Sir."

He let the silence stretch out for a few, tense seconds. "Then get them."

"Sir, we, um …"

James came to our rescue. "Pilot Officers Kent and Hamlin were just dropped off, sir, and their gear has not yet arrived." He took a quick glance over his shoulder. "Their logs are with their gear."

Fulbright shook his head. "What sort of balls-up is

27

this?" Then he looked at me. "How many hours have you logged?"

I did a quick calculation of the time I must have spent playing on the flight simulator. "Three hundred and fourteen."

He looked at Charlie. "And you?"

"The same," Charlie said.

Fulbright's face began to turn red. "What? Are you joined at the hip? How can you expect me to believe you logged the same number of hours?"

"Our training was very similar. Sir," I said.

"And how many of those hours were in a Spitfire?"

We both went silent. I took a breath. "Well—"

"Sir," James said, "there is a bit of a problem."

The crimson in Fulbright's face darkened. "You are not going to tell me, Flight Lieutenant Wyman, that our replacement Spitfire pilots have not flown a Spitfire, are you?"

"If you would rather I didn't," James said, "then I won't."

Fulbright planted his elbows on the desk and rested his chin in his hands. "This, Flight Lieutenant Wyman, is what we call a complete balls-up."

"Yes, sir."

"And what do we do when we run into a complete balls-up?"

"We improvise, sir."

Fulbright picked up his pencil and began marking the chart again. "Then that's what you're going to do. Take these two and show them to Commander Farrow. After he finishes with you, if he doesn't have you shot, come back here with a plan ready."

"A plan, sir?"

"Yes, a plan, on how we are going to get this squadron up to full strength with green replacements who can't fly a Spitfire."

"Yes, sir."

"Now report to Wing Commander Farrow, and for the love of God, don't let him know they aren't experienced pilots."

Chapter 6

Charlie

We left Fulbright and continued up the road, following James. At a branch in the road, near a large, half-painted building labelled "Commissary," James hesitated. The intersecting lane connected with the road leading to Broadbridge Heath. Where the camp ended, however, and blocking access to the road, was a tall gate of timber and barbed wire, manned by two guards.

"I should have a word with them," James said. "Maybe they're as sound asleep as you were when I found you."

"Um, shouldn't we see the Commander first?" Mitch asked.

James glanced towards the gate, where the guards were obviously alert, and then at a tidy cabin at the end of the road. The cabin was wooden, painted military green and set off by itself. The area around it was trim and raked, and a gravel path led from the end of the road to the front door, which was tall and wide and flanked by two soldiers.

James sighed. "I guess it can wait."

I breathed a sigh of relief and we walked on.

We marched up the path with James in front, followed by Mitch, then me. James stopped so abruptly that Mitch nearly ran into him, and I ran into

Mitch. "Flight Lieutenant Wyman reporting to Wing Commander Farrow," he said, standing stiff and staring at a spot somewhere over the door.

The two guards saluted, and one pulled the door open.

The cabin was larger, and grander, inside than it appeared from outside. There were several windows, but all were covered by thick curtains, so the interior was lit by lamps—floor lamps, table lamps, and ceiling lights with proper shades. Most of the lamps sat on, or near, the small tables and dark, wooden chairs set against the walls. The floor was wood and covered with a patterned rug of dark colours. A large mahogany desk dominated the room. It was situated near the far wall, strewn with papers, a wooden In/Out basket, and a telephone, and illuminated by a desk lamp with a green, tasselled shade. There was also a leather cup sprouting various types of pens and pencils, and near the cup was an ink bottle that the skinny man in the blue uniform, who was sitting behind the desk, kept dipping a pen into.

James marched us towards the desk, stopping about ten feet away.

"Flight Lieutenant James Wyman reporting as ordered, sir," he said, saluting in the British manner, with his palm facing out. We stood at attention and saluted like Americans, or Canadians.

The man continued to write for a few moments, then put his pen in the leather-bound cup with the others. Under the glare of the ceiling lights, he looked pale, with a thin, black moustache that drooped over the edges of his mouth. He saluted. We dropped our arms and waited.

"What is the meaning of this?" he asked, after

gazing from Mitch, to me, and then to James, with a look that bordered on contempt.

James remained ramrod straight, staring at a point above the Commander's head.

"The new pilots from Canada, sir."

"I can see that, Lieutenant." His chair squeaked as he leaned forward. "Or, rather, I can't. Where are their insignia?"

"These are our travelling uniforms, sir," I said.

He ignored me and focused on James.

"Travelling uniforms? What sort of poppycock is that? And you were supposed to be here half an hour ago."

"They were delayed, sir."

"No excuse. And why did you not allow them to change into proper uniforms when they arrived?"

"They have no gear, sir."

The chair squeaked again, and the Major leaned back. "No gear? And how in—"

"The army, sir. Temporary delay."

Farrow templed his fingers and rested his chin on them.

"Pilot Officers Kent and Hamlin."

"Sir?" we said, more or less together.

"What do you mean by appearing at my base, late and with no uniforms."

I struggled to come up with an answer and then decided to take James's advice and keep my mouth shut.

"No excuse, sir," Mitch said, staring just above Farrow's head, at the same point James was fixated on.

Farrow continued to glare at us. I felt sweat start to trickle down my back. Then he whipped a sheet of paper from the IN box and began scribbling on it. A few moments later he turned the paper around and laid a pen on it. "Sign these orders."

We walked forward on stiff legs. I took the pen and hoped I could remember who was who. Mitch signed as John Kent, and I signed as Richard Hamlin, and we returned to our positions.

Farrow kept us standing there for a few seconds, his lips curled into a sneer. "Pilots, eh? We'll see about that. Lieutenant Wyman."

"Sir."

"Take these men and get them some uniforms. And assign them bunks. Weiss and Farlow's will do. Dismissed."

We all saluted, but Farrow was already busy with his pen. We about-faced and marched away.

"That when well," James said when we were out of earshot of the guards.

"Really?" I asked. "That was good?"

James smiled. "We were lucky he was busy. If he'd had the time, he would have grilled you. Question after question after question, and I don't think your story would have stood up to much scrutiny."

"He didn't even ask to see any papers," I said.

"All the paperwork has been done," James said, "All that was left was to accept the warm bodies. As you can see, we have enough planes, what we need are experienced pilots."

"But we could have been anyone."

James shook his head and led us towards another Nissan hut. "Who else would you be?"

The next hut was where we were properly processed. Boys in khaki fatigues issued us with several kinds of uniforms—complete with underwear, shoes, boots, belts and ties, and a silk scarf each. And we signed for each and every item, right down to the socks.

The measuring (they said they needed our correct size), the searching, the issuing and the signing took over an hour. Finally, fully loaded, James led us back to the barracks, with us trudging behind him, struggling to hold our bundles. In the long, wooden hut that used to be the home of Edith Pike and her daughter Verdun, James pointed out two bunks next to one another. Unlike the rest of the beds, these had no accompanying furniture. They were simply bare mattresses with sheets and a blanket, folded and stacked in a pile on top of the pillow.

"Welcome to your new home," James said.

Relieved, we tossed our bundles on the beds.

Around the room, some of the pilots looked our way, regarding us with disinterest. Others sat on their beds reading, or were asleep, or just lying on the bunks, silent and staring. One sat at a wooden table near one of the few windows, smoking a pipe. On the table was a telephone that, from time to time, he glanced at as if he was afraid it might bite him.

"We'll requisition some furnishings for you," James said. "In the meantime, you'll have to make do with your footlockers."

I looked to the foot of our beds and saw we each had a green trunk. The trunks had latches, but no locks, and were obviously too small for all the stuff we'd been issued.

James saw me looking. "I'll get you some padlocks," he said.

I looked at the lockers, and then back at our pile of stuff.

"And, if it were me," James added, "I'd keep the most valuable items in your lockers."

He offered a crooked smile and a shrug by way of apology, then said, "Oh, you'll want your blanket back."

He retrieved it from his cabinet and came back, holding it out for me.

I took it from him, hoping he wouldn't notice that it didn't really look like a blanket. He did.

He cocked his head, staring at the cloak as I quickly bundled it up. "That is a strange looking blanket."

I turned to put it on the bed. "It's just—"

"It's a cloak."

I thought it was James talking, but then saw it was a man who appeared behind him. Shorter and stockier than James, he was dressed all in black—black shoes, black suit, black hat—to the point where, if he stood in dim light, you would probably only see his hands and rounded, slightly pink face, floating in the gloom. When his presence became known, all the pilots, James included, stood at attention and saluted.

The man smiled and wafted a hand in front of his face. "No need for such formality, gentlemen. As you were." His soft voice held an edge of authority. "I just stopped by to greet our new arrivals."

The pilots relaxed but continued to glance our way.

I stepped in front of the cloak, trying to hide it from view, but the man in black stepped around me and picked it up.

"So fine," he said, unfurling it and rubbing the material between his thumb and index finger. "But an unusual choice of garment to be travelling with, don't you think?" He looked at me. His lips curled into a smile that didn't register in his black eyes.

"It's ours," I said, a little too forcefully. "Um, I mean, it's Kent's."

The smile widened. "Mmmm. So, you both claim it. Two young men, from the colonies, carrying a cloak. It has an interesting ... echo, don't you think?"

"Mr. Farber, sir," James said. "May I ask why you are interrogating my pilots?"

Farber chuckled and handed the cloak to me. "I do apologize," he said, not to me but to James. "Habit." He looked at Mitch, then at me. "Welcome, gentlemen, to our humble base. What did you say your names were?"

"Pilot Officer Richard Hamlin." The unfamiliar name felt awkward in my mouth, and I hoped he would put it down to nerves.

"Pilot Officer Kent," Mitch said. He managed to sound more natural, but I worried that he had left off his first name because he had forgotten it. I waited for Farber to ask him, but instead he inclined his head slightly towards us, touched the brim of his fedora with an index finger, and walked away as silently as he had come.

When the door closed behind him the barracks seemed to breathe a sigh of relief.

"Head of security," James said. "Intelligence Officer Robinson Farber. He was sent here from the SIS about a week ago."

"SIS?" I asked, laying the cloak on the bed so it looked more like a blanket than a cloak.

"MI6," James said, glancing towards the door. "They call them spooks, and he certainly spooks me."

Mitch opened his locker and began piling stuff in.

I did the same, stuffing the cloak in first, hoping James wouldn't develop an interest in it, or wonder why I was taking it when it was supposed to be Mitch's. From the corner of my eye, I saw him looking at it.

"Maybe you should let me keep that in my locked wardrobe," he said. "If it's that valuable to you, you wouldn't want anything to happen to it."

I handed it to him, still folded neatly like a blanket. He deposited it in his cabinet and came back to us.

"Now, I'm afraid," he said, taking a deep breath, "it's time we went back to see Squadron Leader Fulbright."

Chapter 7

Mitch

"I assume this is your idea of a joke."

Fulbright's face was no longer red, but despite thinking that James had just told him a joke, he wasn't smiling.

"Not at all, sir."

"Two green pilots, who we haven't the facilities, nor the time, to train, and your answer to that is to give the three of you a weekend pass?"

"I have a plan, sir."

Fulbright leaned back in his chair and folded his arms over his chest. "I look forward to hearing it."

James cleared his throat and looked at the two of us, his face a little white.

"These men are experienced pilots," he said, "they simply need to be brought up to speed on the Spitfire. They are familiar with the operations of a Spitfire, and I am convinced, if I am able to school them in groundwork and the finer points of the aircraft, they will be able to fly one."

James took a breath. Fulbright didn't move.

"I will continue their training until I am confident they can handle the aircraft. Then I can show them aerial manoeuvres under the guise of bringing them up to speed on the demands of a fighter squadron. But I need to do it in private, so the other pilots won't know."

Fulbright stared for what seemed a full minute. "Your plan has several flaws. First and foremost, we don't have the time. Secondly, where are you going to conduct this surreptitious training? The morale of this squadron is as stake. It's bad enough as it is, and if my airmen get wind that they've been saddled with two Canadian trainees instead of seasoned fighter pilots, it's going to suffer even more. Commander Follow-Me will have these two shipped out, and you along with them, and where will that leave us?"

James, standing at ease, kept his gaze steady, but I saw his hands, behind his back, clench into fists.

"That's what the weekend pass if for. If I conduct the training in town, no one will know."

Fulbright kept silent for a time, then he leaned forward and clasped his hands on the desk in front of him.

"You still haven't addressed the question of time, of which we have none."

James reddened. "I am confident I will have them flying within the week."

Fulbright shook his head. "Not good enough. Something big is in the works. We need these pilots trained and ready yesterday, not in a week."

I felt my stomach sink. Then Fulbright opened a drawer, pulled out a slip of paper and slapped it on the desk. "One day," he said, scribbling on the paper, "that's all I can give you." He dropped the pen on the desk and held it out to James. "Report back here at seventeen hundred tomorrow with two trained pilots."

James took the paper. "Yes, sir."

Fulbright looked at us. "And you two, you listen to

39

this man. He is one of my most experienced pilots. Failure on your part is not an option, do I make myself clear?"

"Yes, sir," we said.

"And if you so much as put a ding on one of my planes, you won't have to worry about Commander Farrow, because I'll shoot you myself."

I nodded. "Understood, sir." Charlie said nothing.

"Now you've got—"

The sharp clang of the phone cut him off. He snatched up the receiver, knocking his hat aside. He said nothing, just listened, then slammed the phone down. "Scramble," he said. "Full squadron. Bombers with Messerschmitt escorts approaching Folkestone."

"Sections Green and Red are still under manned," James said.

Fulbright looked at us. "You are not taking green pilots up for an intercept. I'm transferring Cook to Green Two."

"But that—"

"Yes, you've only half a flight. I'm assigning Kent and Hamlin to Red. As Red Leader, you can train them. I want them with you. But not yet. Go up as a rover. Now move."

James ran for the door, and we turned to go after him. Then Fulbright bellowed, "Not you two."

"I'm confining you to barracks," he said, as we stepped near the desk and stood to attention. "I don't want Wing Commander Farrow to see you lollygagging around the base. Stay out of sight and say nothing to anyone. Is that clear?"

"Crystal," I said.

We hurried outside and found the previously calm base in a state of controlled pandemonium.

The air men, and others, were stampeding across the green field towards the airplanes. Other men were already at the Spitfires, handing parachutes to the pilots as they arrived, helping them with their flight suits and assisting them into their airplanes. As soon as a pilot was in the cockpit and the canopy closed over him, the engine sputtered, belched smoke, and roared to life. In seconds, the Spitfires inched forward. One by one, they roared past us, bumping over the hard-packed meadow before bouncing into the air and lofting into the grey sky.

I paused to watch, unable to turn away from a sight that was at once riveting and terrifying, until the final plane rose above the perimeter fence and streaked after the others.

Then the base was quiet again. Enlisted men went about their duties. The whine of truck engines replaced the roar of the Spitfires, and the smell of gasoline and exhaust faded. I looked from the perimeter fence to Commander Farrow's office, and then to the Nissan hut of the security unit that Mr. Farber was in charge of. Suddenly, I felt very exposed.

I took a last look at the Spitfires, now dots against the low clouds, flying in formation, up and away, towards some unknown danger. They reminded me of mounted knights, riding into battle.

"We need to go," I said.

Chapter 8

Charlie

In the safety of the barracks, we put our stuff away and dressed in the British Air Force uniforms, which didn't fit us very well. Then we folded our cadet uniforms and put them in the footlockers. We couldn't get everything in them, so we made our beds and stuffed the excess under our pillows, which left them comically high. I kept the Talisman in my pocket. I didn't want it out of my sight.

That took all of forty minutes, and after that we had nothing to do. We thought about lying down on our bunks, but the height of the pillows made that uncomfortable, so instead, we had a look around.

In the centre of the barracks was a pot-bellied stove, along with a small table and a few battered chairs. Nearby was another table, the one we had seen someone sitting at. It had a telephone on it and, next to the phone, a notebook and a pencil. The notebook was open, and the last entry read, "Formation of bombers with Messerschmitt escorts off Folkestone. Squadron scrambled." The date was August 9th, 1940. The previous entry was similar, but had an amendment saying "Squadron returned. No sightings." We looked back a few entries and found another, where the amendment read, "Engaged enemy near coast at Worthing. One Dornier 17 shot down, another damaged. One Messerschmitt damaged. Green Two lost in the Channel. Flight Lieutenant Ken Farlow presumed dead." A few entries further back noted that Flight Lieutenant Tom Weiss had also been shot down.

"Those are the guys whose bunks we have," I said.

Mitch nodded and turned back to the original page. "That's why they needed replacements."

"Yes, but where are they?"

There was no answer to that. All we knew was, when they did show up, we'd be in big trouble.

Then we heard the door open. We thought it was the guys coming back, but we'd heard no planes coming in. Then we saw the silhouette of a man dressed all in black. It was Farber. He slipped silently inside and shut the door behind him.

We ducked down and moved back, towards one of the other bunks. There was a big storage cupboard, like the one James had, next to the bed, and we ducked behind it.

Farber looked around, then went to our bunks. He looked quickly through the stuff under our pillows, pulled back the blankets and searched the beds, then opened our trunks.

"He must think we left with the squadron," Mitch whispered.

"Yes," I whispered back, "but what is he doing here?"

Mitch shrugged and we turned back to Farber, watching.

Slowly, methodically, he removed everything from our trunks, one at a time. He felt every pocket, checked every sock, and then he pulled out our cadet uniforms. After checking the pockets, he held one up, scrutinized it front and back and then looked closely at the shoulders and breast pockets, where the patches had been picked off by mom.

Sweat rolled down my back and I struggled to hold in a sneeze. I was afraid he'd start searching the other bunks, knowing that, if he did, he'd be sure to find us. But all he did was carefully refold everything and put it back just as it had been. Then he closed the trunks, made the beds, and straightened the stuff under our pillows. After a final look around, he left as quietly as he'd come.

"What was that all about?" Mitch asked, still whispering.

"I don't know."

We stayed where we were, not daring to come out in case he returned.

"Do you think he suspects something?"

I let the sneeze out as quietly as I could. "I think he knows we're not who we say we are."

"Do you think he was looking for the cloak?"

"Maybe. But I think it's worse than that. I think he was looking for the Talisman."

There was nothing to do after that but wait. We moved as far away from the door as we could and sat down behind a bunk where we could see the door but would, we hoped, remain hidden.

I leaned back against the wall and tried to stay alert but, eventually, the boredom became too much, and I fell asleep.

The slam of a door jerked me awake and I sat up. Mitch did the same, so I assumed he had been sleeping too.

"Who is it?" Mitch asked.

I peered through the dim light to the far side of

the room. It was one of the pilots, still in a flight suit. He looked around, then pulled off his helmet revealing his red hair.

"James," I said. My knees clicked as I rose.

"What are you blokes doing back there?"

"Hiding," Mitch said, standing up beside me.

"That's a bit extreme, don't you think?"

"Well, we were told to keep out of sight," I said.

James shook his head, then went to his cabinet and unlocked it. "Look, I'm going to shower and change," he said, pulling out a uniform. "Be ready when I get back."

"How did the mission go?" Mitch asked.

James stopped and turned to us. "Not bad. Dogger is wounded, but he'll be all right. Biggins was shot down. He bailed out and I saw him splash down not far from the coast. I'm hoping to get word that he's been picked up."

The way he said it, so nonchalantly, sent a shiver down my spine.

"The others will be here shortly, so get back to your bunks and stop skulking around."

We went towards him as he continued to talk. "Pack light. We'll only be there overnight, so a shirt and underwear if you're fastidious, or nothing if you want to be efficient. And while you're at it …" He pulled the cloak out and tossed it onto Mitch's bunk. "… you should bring that. It will be safer if you keep it with you."

He finished pulling stuff from the cabinet, then shut and locked it.

"I won't be long. I want to get to the house before it gets dark. Then we can start."

"Start what?" I asked.

James faced us, his feet apart, his fresh clothes draped over one arm and his helmet dangling from his hand.

"I'm going to drill you, and drill you, and drill you. And by tomorrow morning you will know your way around a Spitfire blindfolded. And by this time tomorrow, you will have flown one."

Then he about-faced and headed for the door. "Or you will die trying."

The door slammed. I felt myself blanch, but when I looked at Mitch, he was smiling.

Chapter 9

Mitch

The other pilots began drifting in before James returned. They were all in their uniforms, and they all looked a bit dishevelled and tired. They said nothing to us, and we said nothing to them. We just sat on our bunks, with Charlie holding the folded cloak on his lap.

Soon after, James arrived wearing a crisp, new uniform, a cap, and a belt, with a pistol in a brown leather holster.

"Do you think you're going to need that?" Charlie asked, staring at the sidearm.

"No," James said, "I just want to impress my aunt. She remembers the last war. She'll be pleased as punch to see me in this uniform."

I got off the bed and smoothed out the creases in my own uniform. "Your aunt?"

"Yes. She knows I've been stationed here and said I could visit anytime. This is an ideal opportunity, and it will be a great place to do your training."

"I thought we'd be going to a hotel," Charlie said, rising, and cradling the cloak in his arms.

"Too expensive," James said. "The house will do just fine. It will be crowded, but I'm sure we can kip in the sitting room."

"Crowded?" I asked. "Aren't we supposed to be

doing this in secret?"

"It's just my sister, a cousin, and my aunt. They're family," James said. "They can be trusted. Now, if you're ready, we'll go."

He led us out into the late afternoon, and we walked to the main gate, where James showed our pass. They saluted, we saluted, and then we were on the familiar dirt track that led to the little town of Broadbridge Heath. Only the dirt path wasn't dirt, or a path, any longer; it was a wide road topped with gravel, showing the wear of heavy traffic. We followed James, walking past the barracks, which was now on the other side of the fence, and the farmhouse that was still across the lane.

"With luck, we won't have to walk all the way," James said.

I wondered what he meant by that, and the answer came when a battered pickup truck trundled past, churning up gravel and belching smoke. It stopped just ahead of us, and a man with a stubbled beard stuck his head through the open window.

"Going to town?"

James nodded.

"Need a lift?"

"Yes, sir."

"Then hop in."

James gave him a thumbs up and jumped into the back of the truck. We followed, pushing aside some greasy engine parts, and settling down on bales of straw, as the truck lurched and continued bouncing up the road.

I kept an eye on the fence bordering the base. It seemed to go on and on, and when it stopped, buildings began to appear. The base, it seemed, stretched all the way to Broadbridge Heath, or Broadbridge Heath had stretched to meet the base. What had been a tiny settlement was now a town, or at least a village, with houses and stores spreading along the roads in every direction.

We turned onto the old Roman road, heading for Horsham. It didn't take long to get there. Soon, we passed the Green Dragon and the truck slowed as we entered West Street with all the other traffic.

"We'll get out here," James shouted to the driver.

We jumped out, thanked him, and continued up the street, making better time than the truck.

"It's not too far from here," James said, taking the lead.

I tried to keep abreast of him, but he walked fast, and the sidewalk was narrow and crowded. More so than when we had visited in 1916. Mostly, the street looked the same. The buildings hadn't changed, only the businesses, and not all of them. The tobacconists and the shoe store next to it were still there, as was the bakery across the street. Farther up, I saw the drug store—what Annie had called The Chemists—and beyond that, at the junction with South Street, was a familiar, red-brick building advertising itself as Lloyds bank.

He turned there, heading towards the old church and the River Arun.

"Is this where your aunt lives?" Charlie asked from behind.

James glanced at him. "It's not far. Just across the river. And she's not really my aunt, I just call her that. My family used to visit when I was a boy. She was ancient then. But don't worry, she's still spry."

Charlie stopped. "Maggie is still alive?"

James turned to him. "What's that supposed to mean?"

"It's just … well, you said she remembered the last war."

James frowned. "That was only twenty years ago. But, how did you know her name was Maggie?"

"You told us," Charlie said, sounding a little too nonchalant even to me.

"No," James said. "I'm sure I didn't."

"Then how could I know?" Charlie asked.

James shook his head and continues along the street. Charlie came and stood beside me, hugging the cloak to his chest. "You know where we're going, right?"

I nodded. "It's where we always end up, isn't it." I did a quick calculation in my head. "And Maggie would be ninety-seven now, so it all fits. I wonder if the cousin is Annie."

We started walking to catch up to James. "We'll find out soon enough."

I caught up with James, walking next to him, and Charlie came up behind me. Then James asked. "Why did you ask about Aunt Maggie? Why would you think she might be dead?"

His voice carried suspicion and a tinge of anger.

"I didn't mean anything by it," Charlie said. "It's just that you mentioned how old she was."

That bought us a few seconds of silence.

"No, I didn't," James said as we entered the churchyard.

We followed the path to the river.

"I'm sure I recall you saying something," I said, hoping I could convince him.

It seemed to work because he stopped asking.

We came to the foot bridge and crossed, single file. James hesitated, allowing me in front, with Charlie following, and him bringing up the rear. At the other side, I turned down the path to continue along the river to the house. The evening was drawing in and, under the trees, it was getting dark. Charlie walked beside me, both of us eager to get to the house.

Then James called from behind us. "Why is it you know where you're going if you've never been here?"

"Well, it's the only way to go," I said.

"No, it's not," he said, his voice laced with alarm. "You might have turned left, or at least hesitated, but you both just turned this way, as if you know where you're going."

Charlie and I kept walking. James fell further behind.

"It was just a guess," I said, "and you didn't say anything, so I assumed it was the right way."

"No," James said. "You knew. You know. There's something you're not telling me."

The house was just ahead now, looking the same as it had in 1916: a small stone dwelling with a large extension surrounded by a neat lawn and boarded by a stone wall.

"We'll talk about it at the house," Charlie said.

I heard a click.

"No, we won't," James shouted. I turned. He was pointing his pistol at us.

Charlie and I backed up as James came forward. When I got to the gate I stopped and opened it.

"Do not take another step," James commanded.

"If we can just go—"

"You're going nowhere. I'm taking you back to

51

base. You have a lot of questions to answer."

"Look," I said, taking a step down the path towards the house., "we can make it all clear once we get inside."

"One more step and I swear I will shoot," James said.

"James, please," Charlie said, "we just need—"

"That's Flight Lieutenant Wyman to you. And we're going back to base, and you're going to tell me why you know where my aunt lives, and why Farber was so interested in you, and how you got into the Pilots' Quarters without anyone seeing you. And what's with that blanket you keep carrying around. There are a lot of questions needing answers."

He came closer, his arm outstretched with the pistol pointing at my chest. "I'm not even sure you are who you say you are."

I looked at the house and saw a curtain twitch, letting out a stream of yellow light.

"You're right," I said, raising my voice, hoping whoever was at the curtain would hear me. "My name is Mitch Wyman. And he's my brother, Charlie. We're related to you, and we've been sent here on a mission."

James didn't flinch. "You can explain that to Squadron Leader Fulbright. Now move."

"James, Flight Lieutenant Wyman, just let us explain."

"You can explain at the base. Now move or I'll shoot you where you stand."

The door banged open, and a woman ran out. She was middle-aged, with red hair pulled into a bun and wearing a khaki shirt and pants. She ran towards me shouting, "No, James, no."

"Keep away, Annie," James shouted, "these blokes may be spies."

But the woman ignored him. She ploughed into me, enveloping me in an embrace, her back to James, between me and the pistol. "Oh Mitch, Mitch," she said, her face against my cheek, "I knew you'd come back." She continued hugging me like she never wanted to let go. I felt tears running down my neck.

"Get away, Annie," James shouted, "get away now."

Then another woman came through the door. An old woman with white hair and a cane. She moved sprightly down the path, passed by us, and grabbed Charlie around the shoulders with her free arm. Then she looked at James. "Put that thing away, Jimmy, these boys are our friends."

Chapter 10

Charlie

"I'm still … I don't …," James said.

He was sitting at the end of the table, with a white face and, thankfully, without his gun. Annie had put it in her bedroom, along with our cloak.

They had been sitting down to eat when we arrived, so they found a few more chairs and had us join them. Mitch was sitting on a bench with Annie, who kept beaming at him. I sat in a wooden chair next to Emma, whose face was also a bit white, which made her freckles and red hair stand out. Her hair was cut short, about shoulder length, and pulled back with a big clip. She wore a canvas shirt and rugged pants with dirt stains on them. Her heavy shoes were also caked with dirt. Maggie, dressed in a flannel shirt and long skirt, sat at the other end of the table, looking from me to Mitch, and then at James.

"Just eat," she said. "You'll feel better if you're doing something normal."

I didn't need to be told twice. I hadn't eaten since breakfast, so I dug into the stew. I noticed it didn't have any meat in it, but it was good, nonetheless.

"These boys first visited me," she continued between bites, "in 1851, when your great-grandfather John brought them to my house."

James who was bringing a spoonful of stew to his

mouth, put it back down. "1851?"

"And they came again in 1916," Annie said, gazing again at Mitch. "They were ever so brave. They shot down a zeppelin."

James's next bite was again thwarted. "A zeppelin?"

"Yes," Maggie said, "regular heroes, they were."

"But how——"

"In that BE2c I told you about," Mitch said. "I really can fly."

"These are the boys you told me about?" Emma asked, looking at Annie. "The knights from long ago? Brothers, travelling with a cloak?"

"Yes," Annie said. "Their stories have been handed down from mother to daughter since, oh, I don't know when."

"Yes, you told me," Emma said, her face going even whiter, "but I didn't believe it."

Annie laughed. "Neither did I, but you can't deny it now."

"But they're just pilots, like Jimmy, you can't know——"

"I do," Annie said. "I was with them. They came to me, with the cloak. But I understand how you feel. I was taken aback, just like you are now."

"Taken aback? I'm … I …"

"Eat, child," Maggie said. "You need to keep your strength up."

Emma took a few mouthfuls of stew, and the colour began to return to her face.

We ate in silence for a while, then James laid his spoon down. "If you're knights from the ancient times, when was that? And how old are you?"

"It's not like that," Mitch said. "We're not one of

the immortals—"

"Immortals!" James said.

"We're travellers, from the future," Mitch continued. "The cloak brings us to where we're needed, and when."

"But how—"

"We don't know," Mitch said, "it's as surprising to us as it is to you."

"And what are you here for this time?" Maggie asked.

"If you're from the future," James cut in, "then you know who won the war."

The room went silent. I drew a breath. "It's not that simple. In our world, we won. But it seems time can be split. There is a future where the Germans win, and the consequences are terrible. We're here to stop that."

"How?" Annie asked, placing a hand on Mitch's shoulder. "You're not going to do something dangerous, are you?"

"I don't think so," I said, pulling the Talisman from my pocket and holding it up for them to see. "I believe all we need to do is put this back where it belongs."

"Is that the Talisman?" Maggie asked. "John told me about that. What's it for?"

"It's an ancient stone," I said, turning it so the light reflected on its surface. It was now back as I remembered it, unmarred and smooth as a mirror. "It's made of Star Fire, and it holds great power. There is a tor, and inside it is a temple, and it needs to be put back there. The last time we were here, Mer … the Druid, told us that as long as the Talisman was in its receptacle, no harm could come to the Land." I left out the part about Arthur and Merlin, thinking that would be too much for them.

James shook his head. "That is just … this is … who's the Druid?"

"He's the immortal," Mitch said. "We first met him in Roman times, and he was still alive in 1916."

"That can't be," Emma said. "No one can live that long. It must be different people."

"That's what you find hard to believe?" James asked.

"He looks the same every time we see him," I said. "He has a scar on his right cheek that runs up around his eye, like a question mark. And each time we come, he helps us. But when we were here in 1916, he was … not well. People don't believe in the Talisman anymore, and I think it made him fade away. He made it clear to me then that we were on our own now."

I put the Talisman back in my pocket and silence descended again. We ate slowly, everyone grappling with the extraordinary revelations in their own way.

"Where is this tor?" Annie asked.

"I've been thinking about that," Mitch said. "When we were, you know, home, I did some searching, and I think it's the place you call Glastonbury."

"If that's the case," Annie said, "you could take the morning train to London and then out to Glastonbury. You could be there well before nightfall." She paused and looked at James. "Jimmy can go with you. He'll be able to help you with the trains."

James looked up, an incredulous expression on his face. "I'm not going anywhere. You can't expect me to believe all this."

Maggie rose from her chair. "I suppose it is all a bit much. Let me show you something that might help."

She walked slowly away from the table and down the hallway. We waited. No one spoke, or ate, or breathed. She returned a few minutes later, holding an old piece of parchment, rolled up and tied with a faded, red ribbon. She walked to where James sat and handed the paper to him. He looked at her, confused.

"Read it," she said.

James untied the ribbon and unrolled the parchment. It crinkled as he pulled it to its full length. His eyes moved back and forth as he scanned the writing, his mouth slowly dropping open as he read. "It's a royal pardon, for Mitch, Charlie and John Wyman, signed by Queen Victoria."

He lowered the paper. "What in the seven hells is this about?"

"I got that paper from your great-grandfather, John," Maggie said. "That pardon has not been opened in over seventy years. Ask them what it says."

James looked at Mitch.

"We were pardoned for saving the life of their daughter, Princess Victoria."

"And they awarded us a hundred pounds," I added.

"And it's dated the first of May 1851," Mitch said.

Maggie took the paper from James's shaking hands. It snapped back into a roll, and she wrapped the ribbon around it.

James shook his head in disbelief. "A hundred pounds?"

"Yes," Maggie said. "Each. Mitch and Charlie gave

theirs to my mother. How do you think we were able to buy this house?"

James slumped back in his chair, looking confused and defeated.

"It's settled, then," Annie said. "You'll leave first thing in the morning."

"What? And go AWOL? Besides, I'm supposed to spend the day teaching them to fly."

Annie shook her head. "There won't be any need for that. When you get back, you can return to the barracks, and they can go home."

"Don't you get it?" James asked. "If we're not back by seventeen hundred tomorrow we'll be listed as absent without leave or, worse, deserters. Are you trying to get me shot?"

"That won't be necessary," I said, looking at Mitch. "Remember last year, when we were at the Tor? We were able to get back from there."

"That's right," Mitch said, looking at James. "Charlie and I can go out, just the two of us. You can go back and report us missing. That will keep you in the clear, and by the time they start looking for us, we'll be gone.

"Besides," I said. "If the real Kent and Hamlin show up, that won't be good for any of us."

James shook his head. "This is too—"

"I'll go with you," Annie said. She looked at Mitch, her eyes bright. "I've waited so long for you, I can't bear to think of you leaving so soon, without me being with you for at least a little while."

James covered his face with his hands. "This is really too much."

"I'll go, as well," Emma said. Everyone, except James, looked at her in surprise. "Annie got to have an adventure with them. I want one, as well."

Maggie laughed. "I don't suppose there's any problem with that."

"Wonderful," Annie said. "We'll all have an adventure together."

Mitch nodded, but I didn't feel good about it. I felt like I should say something, but before I could speak, there was a rap on the door and a young woman, dressed in a khaki jacket, knee-length khaki skirt, and with a black World War One-style helmet on her head, stepped inside.

"Sorry," she said, "but you've got light showing through your front window."

Annie jumped up and went into the living room to adjust the dark curtain. "Apologies, Mrs. Marsh. It was well-covered earlier. I must have moved it to look outside when our company arrived."

The woman waved her hand. "No, my apologies. I didn't know you were entertaining. I would have been a little more discreet."

"Verdy," Maggie said, "you've come at just the right time. Do you recall the story your mother told you, about when your house was bombed?"

Verdy blushed. "Really," she said, "I don't think these young men want to hear that."

I looked at Maggie. She gave me a wink and I suddenly realized who Verdy was, and what Maggie wanted me to do. I stood up and took a step towards the woman.

"No," I said. "We don't need to hear it. We know all about it. We were there. We're the ones who saved you."

Verdy's face went from red to white so fast I was afraid she would pass out. "You're the angels?"

60

Behind me, James groaned. "Now they're angels?"

Verdy came towards me. I stepped forward and met her halfway. She threw her arms around me and squeezed. "Mother told me about you so often. You've always been real to me, but I never thought I would ever see you."

"We're not angels, though," I said, extracting myself from her embrace.

"You're angels to me. Mother would be so thrilled."

"Would you like to see the cloak?" Maggie asked.

Verdy looked away from me to Maggie. "Oh, I would give the earth to see it, but I've got my rounds. Can I come back, and visit properly when I'm off duty?"

"Of course," Maggie said.

Verdy embraced me again, then slowly pulled away, touching my arms and face as if she was afraid I'd disappear. "Thank you. Thank you. I'll come back. Soon. Please say you'll still be here."

I nodded. "We will."

She backed up, her face still white. "I … I'll … until later."

She left then, pulling the door closed behind her. Everyone looked at James.

James looked around, baffled. "Am I the only one having trouble believing this?"

No one spoke. He heaved a big sigh. "I guess I'll have to go along with it, then."

Chapter 11

Mitch

"Does everyone in the squadron have a nickname?" I asked.

We were in the sitting room having tea. I was on the couch with Annie close to me. Maggie was in a cushioned chair, while James, Emma and Charlie were facing us across the coffee table, sitting in chairs we had taken from the dining room. It was strange, being so close to Annie again. I hadn't stopped thinking about her, but she was so different now, a grown woman. But oddly, I still felt drawn to her. To distract me, and James, who still looked a little peaked, we were attempting to make normal conversation.

"Most do," James said.

"Why do they call you 'Red'? Is that because you're Red Leader?"

James shook his head. "No, it's because of my hair. I got it the first day I arrived."

No one said anything else, so I pressed on. "Will we have nicknames?"

"You're not assigned a nickname when you join up," James said, finally warming to the subject, "you earn it. The others, they'll give you one. If you're accepted."

Now I went silent. I knew what he meant. We'd have to prove ourselves worthy of becoming one of the group, something that wasn't going to happen.

"Do you remember the feather I gave you?" Annie asked to ease the silence.

"Yes," I said, "I do."

"It came back with us," Charlie said. "The only thing that ever returned. That's when we realized all this was really happening. Up until then, we thought we'd been having strange dreams."

"You still have it?" Annie asked, surprised.

Charlie laughed. "He sure does. He keeps it on his dresser and moons over it."

Annie blushed. She looked at me, her green eyes shining. I felt myself flush.

"How sweet," Emma said.

I cleared my throat and looked away from Annie. "The Wing Commander, Farrow. Is his nickname Follow-Me?"

This made James chuckle. It was good to see. "Don't ever call him that to his face," he said. "Farrow was a platoon commander during the Great War, and rumour has it he used to shout, 'Follow me' as his men went over the top. Only he'd be the last one out."

I nodded. "Yes, I get it now."

"He also had a reputation for shooting deserters and malingerers, which was why Fulbright joked about him shooting you. He's itching to pick up the practice again, but the military isn't keen to go down that route in this war, much to Old Follow-Me's dismay."

"But he's in the RAF now," Charlie said. "Did he quit the army and join the air force?"

"No. He joined the Royal Flying Corps, which was part of the army, midway through the war. He was, by all accounts, a good pilot. Near the end of the war, the Royal Flying Corps and the Royal Navy Air Service were combined into the RAF. As a decorated pilot, he worked his way up through the ranks. And now we've been lumbered with him."

I drank the last of my lukewarm tea and put the dainty cup in its saucer on the table. "Not the best commander in the service?"

James shrugged. "Well, at least you won't have to worry about him."

The mood of the room began to lighten. Even James seemed more relaxed. Then the door opened.

We all looked up, expecting the return of Verdy. But Farber stepped into the room, with a revolver in his hand.

"Well, well," he said in his soft voice, "look who we have here."

James, Charlie, and I jumped to our feet, but he pointed the gun at us, and we froze.

"In a hurry to die?" he asked, gently closing the door behind him. He waved the gun, pointing to the middle of the room. "Everyone, on your knees, facing me, your hands locked behind your heads."

We continued to rise but Farber pointed the gun at us again. "Your knees! Now! Crawl."

We got on our knees and shuffled into a group. "Not Aunt Maggie," James said.

Farber paced, still near the door, tapping the pistol against his thigh. "If you mean the old lady, she's not exempt. Everyone."

"It's okay," Maggie said, getting to her knees and inching forward. "Just stay calm. Everything will be all right."

Farber smiled at this. When we had assembled into

a cluster, he stepped a little closer, pointing the gun at Charlie and then at me. "You two," he said. "I must admit I'm a little amazed. I was beginning to doubt my Führer. But then you appeared."

"Führer," James said. "Then you're not an intelligence officer."

"Oh, but I am," Farber said. "But that doesn't mean I'm not loyal to the Fatherland."

"What are you talking about?" Charlie asked.

"I suppose," Farber said, rubbing his chin with his free hand, "there is no harm in telling you the story. It may encourage you to help me, rather than forcing me to rely on less pleasant methods."

He cleared his throat and began pacing in front of us, his hand clasped behind his back, still holding the gun. "The Führer is a man of genius who is not afraid to explore unorthodox methods in order to hasten our Reich's destiny. In his wisdom, he had our best minds—researchers, mystics, historians—scouring your legends to probe your national psyche, and in doing so, he discovered tales of a magic stone called the Talisman."

I couldn't conceal my look of surprise and, apparently, neither could Charlie, because Farber stopped in front of him with a satisfied smile on his face.

"The tales tell of two young men, who come bearing a cloak, and who are tasked with assisting this stone. I thought it rather too fanciful, I confess, but then you arrived, with a cloak."

I said nothing, I just looked for an opportunity. That was going to be difficult, as I was in the back row with Annie and Maggie. Emma, Charlie and James were kneeling in front of me, so there was no way I could move. Plus, it would be awkward getting out of the position I was in, which I assumed was why he had us kneeling that way. Farber continued to look at Charlie, standing temptingly close, but there was nothing he could do, either.

"A fanciful idea," Farber said, now facing us with his hands back at his sides and the gun, once again, tapping on his thigh, "and yet, perhaps unknown to the Führer, or perhaps something his genius had revealed to him, I had, unwittingly, already heard of you. Two young men, boys, really, who appeared from nowhere, and shot down one of our Zeppelins."

That name, I thought: Farber. "You're related to Captain Farber" I said. "The spy."

Farber nodded. "My father," he said. "A loyal German. Someone you would call a sleeper agent, like myself. He sacrificed much to work his way into a position where he could assist the Fatherland. He should have returned a hero. But he returned in disgrace, a broken man." He shoved the gun at Charlie, ramming it against his forehead. "Because of you."

I felt the blood drain from my face. "It was war," I shouted. "We were on opposite sides. We did our duty, just as he did."

Farber let out a long breath and lowered the gun. Then he backed away. "He wouldn't speak of it," he said, "for years. But eventually he told me. The boys, and a rumour of a cloak. No mention of this magic stone, though. I didn't believe it, of course, but when I saw you, I remembered my father's words, and the orders of my Führer." Farber raised the revolver, pointing it upward, and tapped the end of the barrel against his temple. "Now I'm thinking, who knows, the Führer may be on to something."

He stepped back and pointed the gun at us, aiming at each of us in turn. "If the legends are true, you're here to take the stone, the Talisman, to the Tor at Glastonbury. But I'm here to take it from you and bring it to my Führer. Now where is it?"

"The bedroom," I said. "It's in the bedroom."

Farber looked towards the hall. He now had a problem. He couldn't leave us to go look for it, and if he sent me to get it, I'd come back with a gun. Although he didn't know that.

Farber pondered a few moments, then he came forward, in quick, easy strides and grabbed Emma by the hair. She squealed in pain as he dragged her towards him. He held her head sideways against his thigh and jammed the gun in the back of her neck.

"The old woman goes," he said. "And she will step back into this room with her hands high above her head and the stone in one of them. If she does not, I will shoot the girl."

My heart sank. It was over now. Then Charlie said, "Don't hurt her. I have it. Here. In my pocket."

Farber nodded to him, still holding the gun against Emma. Charlie dug in his pocket and pulled the Talisman out.

"Slide it to me," Farber ordered.

Charlie slid the Talisman. It skidded over the floorboards. Farber stopped it with his foot.

"A wise move," he said. Then he pushed Emma away. She scuttled to Charlie, who grabbed her. She wrapped her arms around him, her face pressed to his neck as she shuddered and moaned.

Farber picked up the Talisman. He gazed at it, still pointing the gun in our direction. "At last," he said.

"The Führer believes that, without this, the British cannot win the war, and with it, Germany cannot lose." He gazed at the ebony surface. "And I am beginning to believe him."

I waited for his face to go slack. It would tell me if the Talisman was speaking to him. If it did, he would fall into a trance. For how long, I couldn't say. I would simply have to be ready. I waited, but his eyes didn't glaze over; he remained alert and the Talisman remained closed to him.

He shoved it into the side pocket of his jacket, then aimed the gun at us again.

"You have what you came for," James said. "Now leave."

Farber smiled. "Oh, I see you don't understand. I can't leave any witnesses. There can't be anyone on my tail as I arrange my departure." He held the revolver in front of his face and gazed at it. "Hmm, six people, and six bullets. It's like it was meant to be. The only question is, in which order? Youngest to oldest, or vice versa?"

He came closer and pointed the gun at Charlie and Emma. "You two lovebirds break it up. Who wants to go first?"

No one moved. Then there was a rap at the door and Verdy entered, still wearing her uniform and helmet. "Sorry to come so late but I was held … oh."

Farber stepped to the middle of the room and pointed the gun at her. "You've just changed the equation," he said. "I now have more people than bullets. I suppose that means I should go youngest to oldest. I can certainly take care of the old lady without the help of a revolver."

He held the gun on Verdy, motioning her to join

our group. She took a step towards him and began raising her hands. Then she shouted, "Not on my watch, you don't!" and whipped her helmet off, flinging it at Farber.

Chapter 12

Charlie

While she'd had her face buried in my neck, Emma had whispered, "He can't shoot us both. On my signal, jump him. I'll go left, you go right."

When Farber made her pull away, I looked at her with a mixture of awe and fear. I got myself ready, but before she gave a signal, Verdy was there, and a helmet was flying through the air.

The helmet hit him in the temple, knocking his hat off. He jerked backward. A gunshot rang out. The bullet struck the ceiling above Verdy's head. The sound clapped against my ears, nearly deafening me, wrenching a memory from the back of my mind so sharply I was momentarily stunned.

"Now!" Emma shouted.

I was half a second behind her. She hit him first. He stumbled but didn't fall and brought the gun around towards her. I dived at his legs, and he fell to the floor. Another shot went off, into the wall this time. The room filled with screams and the smell of cordite.

Farber had fallen on me and I struggled to get out from under him. Emma grabbed the helmet and hit him on the head with it. His gun hand dropped towards the floor. I grabbed his wrist, pounding his hand against the floorboards until the pistol slipped from his fingers. I batted it away and it went under the couch.

James was up now. I saw him from the corner of my eye. Farber, blood oozing from his head where the helmet had hit him, grabbed Emma and, with his free arm, launched her at James. They both tumbled to the floor and Mitch tripped over them. Farber kicked and thrashed and struggled to his feet. I grabbed for him and got my hand on his coat pocket. He took a shambling step forward with me holding onto him, then his pocket ripped open. The talisman clinked to the floor and rolled away. Annie scooped it up and Farber continued to run. He ploughed into Verdy, pushed her aside and ran out the door.

Me and Emma and Mitch and James ran after him, but by the time we were out on the path, he was gone, swallowed up by the night.

Back inside we shut and bolted the door.

"The shutters," James said.

We ran into the sitting room, threw aside the heavy curtains, opened the windows, and pulled the shutters closed. They were thick oak, with sturdy metal latches. No one was going to get through them in a hurry, not without making a racket. Then we went to the kitchen, and down the hall to the bedrooms and bathroom, closing the rest. When we finished, we returned to the sitting room. Annie was there, still sitting on the floor. She looked up when we came in and stretched her hand out with the Talisman resting on her palm.

"You need this," she said.

I put it in my pocket and helped her to her feet. Verdy came to her side. "We have to report him," she said. "I'll go to my commander."

"And I'll go to mine," Annie said.

"Fulbright needs to know," James said, "and Farrow. They'll organize a manhunt. He won't get far."

I struggled through the fog of thoughts in my head. "No," I said. Everyone looked at me, stunned.

"We can't afford to start a big investigation," I said. "We'll get caught up in it. We need to be free to move."

They all continued to stare at me, none of them looked convinced. Then Maggie came out of the kitchen with a ceramic tea pot and another cup and saucer. "Let's all sit down and discuss this rationally, now, shall we?"

Maggie poured more tea. We passed around the milk and sugar and I took the time to organize my thoughts.

"We're safe from Farber for the moment," I said. "He can't go back to the base for help. Not only will he assume we turned him in, he can't afford an investigation any more than we can. Think about it. Farber could have spun some story about us being traitors or something. He could have shown up here with a dozen armed MPs. But he didn't. He came here alone because, if he didn't, we'd have been arrested and incarcerated and out of his control. He doesn't want us, he wants the Talisman. And we don't need to catch him, we need to get the Talisman to the Tor." I drew a breath and took a sip of tea. "He's out there, alone, wounded, and unarmed. He'll go to ground and regroup. Then he'll come after us again. We need to be gone before he can do that."

"So, what's your plan?" James asked.

"Same as before. Sort of." I looked at Maggie.

"We'll need to make sure Maggie is safe and the four of us will leave as early as possible for the Tor. James can go back to the base in the afternoon and report us missing, but by then it should be over."

James looked sceptical. "I don't know."

"I'll take Maggie home with me," Verdy said. "She'll be safe there."

"Should we go now?" Maggie asked.

"I think we need to stay here for the night," Mitch said. "If any of us leave, Farber might track us. He's nearly invisible in the dark."

"So, what, we just wait?" James asked. "What if he comes back?"

"We're seven to one with two guns," Maggie said. Then she looked at Verdy. "And a very handy helmet."

"We'll still need to be vigilant," Mitch said. "I'll take the first watch."

◆

There were only two bedrooms in the house, so we turned them into the Girls' dorm and the Boys' dorm. We dragged the couch into Maggie's room and she, Annie and Emma bunked down in her big bed while Verdy slept on the couch. Me and Mitch and James slept in Annie's room. Her bed wasn't as big but there were only two of us in it at a time. Mitch went on watch with Farber's revolver, and James slept with his own pistol close by on the nightstand.

James took the second watch, then it was my turn. I put my clothes on and settled into the cushioned chair, which we had positioned near the front door, holding Farber's revolver in my lap.

A single lamp burned in the sitting room, casting a dull glow. The rest of the house was dark and silent. It was four in the morning, and soon the sky would lighten into a murky dawn. I had an hour before I could put my plan into action. So, I waited.

When it was nearly five o'clock, I stood up, stretched, and turned around to find Annie standing behind me. I almost yelped in surprise.

"Sorry," she whispered. "I couldn't sleep. I thought I'd come and keep you company."

This was not something I had planned on or wanted, but I nodded to her, and she got one of the dining chairs and set it next to mine. We settled in, waiting, with me wondering how I was going to get rid of her.

"Also," Annie said, in a quiet voice, "I thought it would be best to have someone on guard duty after you left."

I turned to her. "What?"

"You're planning to leave," she said. A statement, not a question. "I can take over your watch." She smiled. "That way, James won't have to shoot you for desertion."

"But how … why?"

She continued to look at me, saying nothing.

"The Talisman," I said. "You saw something in it." She nodded.

"What?"

"What I needed to see."

"So …"

"I don't know much. All I know is that Mitch needs to stay here. That means you're going to the Tor alone." She glanced towards the hallway. "You'd better move quick. Maggie will be awake soon. She's quite the early bird."

"What about you?" Then I thought about how Mitch would feel finding me gone. "And Mitch?"

Annie laid a hand on my arm. "I'll tell him. He'll understand. Now go."

I handed her the gun. "Do you know how to use this?"

She smiled again. "Don't worry."

The cloak was still in Maggie's room. I tiptoed down the hall and pushed the door open. As near as I could tell in the darkness, they were all asleep. The cloak was draped over the end of the couch, which was next to the door. I lifted it, quietly, and backed into the hall. No one stirred.

Back in the sitting room I folded it into a bundle like Ellen had taught me. I did it quickly. The bundle was loose and would come apart soon but that wasn't as urgent as getting away. I unbolted the door and put my hand on the doorknob.

"Don't you want the pistol?"

She held it out to me. I shook my head. "It will be more trouble than it's worth."

She laid the gun on her chair and pulled me to her, hugging me tight. In my mind, I saw her as the brave, obnoxious, resourceful young girl who had beguiled my brother, and hugged her back.

"You'll need a coat," she whispered.

"No," I said, my voice muffled against her shoulder. "It will get warm once the sun comes up."

She held me for a few more seconds as I burned with impatience.

"Be safe," she whispered. I nodded and pulled away.

The door squeaked as I opened it, making me

wince. When it was wide enough, I slipped into the grey dawn. The door closed behind me, the latch clicked into place, and I was alone.

I stood silent, breathing in the crisp air. The birds had not begun to greet the dawn, which was still a while off. It was so peaceful and still I could hear the babble of the River Arun. I stepped over the wall, thinking it would make less noise than opening the gate. On the path, I headed for the foot bridge. That would be the best place for an ambush. I moved cautiously, constantly looking, straining to see in the murky light.

By the time I crossed the bridge and navigated through the churchyard, dawn was truly breaking, and I realized I was running late. I'd left at five o'clock, assuming the streets would be deserted, making it harder for Farber to sneak up on me. But West Street and the Carfax, instead of being silent and empty, were bustling with people. The Bakers on West Street were already open, and lights were on in most of the other shops. The Saturday market in the Carfax wasn't doing business yet, but the stallholders were all there, setting up and arranging their products. A babble of voices and the sound of vehicles and horses filled the dawn.

I hurried past, heading for the road that led to the station. It was later than I thought. I wanted to catch the first train and I didn't know when that would be, but I was beginning to fear I might miss it. As I left the Carfax, a shadowy figure stepped from behind a building. I jumped aside, preparing to run.

"No," the figure said, beckoning to me. "In here, quick!"

The voice sounded more urgent than threatening. I

followed the figure into the shadows, zigging and zagging around bushes and trees. Near a brick wall, bordering the road, we stopped. The figure turned. It was Emma.

"What do you think you're doing?" I hissed.

"I'm coming with you," she said.

"No, you're not."

She shook her head. "You need me." Her hair was tucked up under a cap, giving her a masculine look. She wore a canvas shirt with a pair of heavy pants, and the same shoes I had first seen her in. On her back was a pack, stuffed full, and in one hand she carried another that appeared to be empty.

"That's absurd!"

She stood straight and put her hands on her hips. Then she pointed at the cloak, which was beginning to unravel. "Oh? What have you there?"

"The cloak."

She threw the empty pack at me. "Put it in this kit bag. You'll look strange wearing a fancy uniform and carrying a field pack, but at least you won't look like a hobo."

I began doing as she said. "Okay. But you're still not coming with me. It's too dangerous."

"You won't get far without me," she said. "You may be able to get around in whatever time you come from, but you know sweet FA about 1940."

"I got along well enough in the Middle Ages," I said, trying to keep my voice down.

"Well, Annie told me how hopeless you were in her time, and—"

"Annie? Did she put you up to this?"

"No. She just knew I wanted to go, and she knew you were going to sneak off unprepared, so she helped me pack last night, and she distracted you this morning so I could sneak out the bathroom window."

It all came together, the coming to sit with me, the long good-bye, and me rushing out without thinking. I had so many questions to ask, but all I could think of was: "What did you pack?"

"Food, water, a torch. You know, useful things. And this." She reached into her pocket and pulled out a few pieces of paper. "Money. Do you have any?"

It was all I could do to not slap myself on the forehead.

She put the bills back in her pocket. "If you still think you don't need me, then go your own way. Otherwise, come with me."

She turned and headed into the shadows. I slung the pack on my back and followed, walking quickly to catch up with her.

We hurried through the greenery behind the wall, crouching low and running. When we got to the end, we stayed low and moved from bush to bush until we had a view of the station. It was getting light enough to see now, and I noted that the station didn't look like it had in 1916. It was now a low, brick building, relatively new. I could see train carriages on the track behind it, but no smoke.

"Looks like I'm on time, at least."

"What do you mean by that?" Emma asked, not taking her eyes off the station.

"If the steam engines were starting—"

"Steam engines? We use electric now. What, do you think this is 1850 or something?"

"Well, I guess—"

"You didn't know. And you'd have walked right into that station expecting a steam engine and a ticket without any money to pay for it."

"Okay," I said, rising. "Point taken. You can come with me."

She grabbed my arm and pulled me back down.

"Hey!"

"Shh! Watch. Look. Tell me what you see."

I peered through the bush. There were people of all types going into and out of the station. Cars, trucks, horses and carriages passed by, some dropping off passengers or employees. A few men in work clothes stood outside, smoking hand-rolled cigarettes.

"I see that it looks safe," I said.

Emma nodded. "Sure, except for those guys smoking, who have been paid by Farber to grab you when you arrive. Farber himself is waiting inside the station."

I ducked further behind the bush. "How could you know that."

"You said he'd try to pick you up at the Tor, because that's where he knows you're going. But he also knows that to get there, you most likely need to catch a train."

"But you don't know—"

"I got here before you did. I saw Farber paying those men. Then I went back to intercept you."

I felt utterly defeated.

"Okay then," I sighed, "what do we do now?"

"We go to another station."

"Which one?"

"See," she said, "you don't know that either. Follow me."

Chapter 13

Mitch

"Once more," James said. "Do it again."

We were in the kitchen. I was sitting in a chair, facing James, who was sitting in another chair about three feet away, facing me. I reached in front of me and made a pretend grab. "This is the stick." I pointed with my other hand. "Here is where the landing gear lever is. I raise and lower the wheels by pumping it."

"And how do you know if they are up or down?"

I pointed a little to my left. "Landing gear indicator is here."

When we had awakened early in the morning to find Annie on guard duty and Charlie gone, I was livid. Not only had he abandoned me, but he'd left me no way to get home. Then James had found his sister gone and he became livid too. Annie sat us down and gave us a talking to and I finally accepted that he'd done the right thing. James took longer to come around, but when I sided with Annie, agreeing that Charlie needed someone to act as a guide for him, he became a little calmer.

Then we had to form a new plan, and that involved him taking me back to the base to fly the Spitfire and report Charlie as missing.

James remained sceptical about the chances of that

working until I had us sit in the chairs and point out, from memory, all the components of the Spitfire's cockpit.

"Up here," I said, moving my finger to the upper centre, "is the airspeed gauge, attitude, climb, altitude, heading, and the Turn-Slip indicator."

"All right," James said, "you know what it looks like. Do you know how to fly it? Take off for me."

I took a breath. "Okay, I get in the plane—"

"How?"

"Um, there's a door."

"Which side?"

"Left."

"Port!"

"Okay. I climb up on the port side wing, open the hatch and slide into the cockpit."

"Wearing…?"

"My parachute? And a flight suit'"

James smiled. "Parachute for sure. Your flight suit is called a Sidcot suit, and you'll have your helmet and mask. Plus, your silk scarf, unless you want a raw neck."

I nodded. "Okay, I've settled in. Now I put the harness on and lock it with the lock pin. Next, I put on my helmet, goggles, and mask, and attach the Radio Transmitter cable and oxygen supply."

"Where?"

I pointed to my right. James nodded. I leaned forward, flicking an imaginary switch. "Master on," I said, "now I check the fuel gauge and oxygen. The undercarriage indicator should be green, for down. Flaps switch up, landing lights up, both fuel levers up."

I continued the narrative, adjusting the elevator

trim, setting the gyro, opening the throttle, calling "All Clear?" to the ground crew and then "Contact" to begin my taxi. I started the imaginary airplane, adjusted the controls, rolled it forward to the runway, lined up, increased the throttle, and pretended to lift off the ground.

James watched me the whole time, leaning back in his chair, his arms folded across his chest. When I finished, he gave a quick nod. "Congratulations" he said. "You've just crashed."

I felt my cheeks redden. "Well, if I had been in a real plane—"

"If you had been in a real Spitfire, you'd be dead, if you were lucky. If not, you'd be in a world of trouble."

"So, what didn't I do—"

He leaned forward, taking over his own imaginary cockpit. "First of all, you didn't check with the ground crew to see that they acknowledged you were ready. You do nothing without checking with your ground crew. And to start the Spitfire, you press the starter button, then push in the priming pump handle, and hold the two until the Merlin engine fires up smoothly. That's important. If you spot flames, that means you flooded the engine. In that case, hold the starter button in until the flames clear, otherwise, your plane will catch fire."

I nodded and he continued.

"Watch the temperature gauge, especially on a hot day while you are sitting still. The Merlin engine will overheat quickly, and you cannot, repeat, cannot allow the temperature to exceed one hundred degrees centigrade, so taxi as soon as possible and keep checking the temperature until take off. Check that your cockpit door is locked in the half-open safety position and that the cockpit hood is locked in the open position. Now, you cannot see the ground in front of you at all because the engine is in the way, so you need to swerve from side to side to avoid running into anything."

He continued his monologue detailing a hundred different things I had missed.

"When you're ready for take-off, don't hang about or it will overheat. You need to get airborne as quickly as you can. A good run is about two-hundred and thirty yards, which should take just under ten seconds. Be prepared to move your right foot forward for full right rudder to counteract the swing effect of the engine. At about forty miles per hour, the tail will lift level with the plane. Do not push the control column too far forward at this point as it could force the nose down and damage the plane. Now, work both the right aileron and the right rudder to keep the Spitfire running in a straight line. Increase power. At eighty-five miles per hour your plane will rise into the air. Hold steady on the control column and feel the lift. Do not start to climb until you are at one hundred and forty. A normal rate of climb is achieved at one hundred and eighty-five."

James grinned at the panicked expression on my face.

"As all this is going on, ease off the right rudder and move your left hand off the throttle lever to the control column and your right hand to the undercarriage control lever. Press the brake to stop the wheels from spinning and raise the undercarriage until it locks into place. Listen for the two bumps that tell you the wheels are up. You can confirm this by checking the indicator has turned from green to red."

I put my hand up to stop him. "Okay, I get it. I'm not ready to fly a Spitfire."

James shook his head. "I wouldn't say that. I'm dead impressed by this simulator, as you call it. Your knowledge is good. There are a few holes in it, but nothing we can't fill. It's the practical experience you lack."

"Well," I said, "you can only do so much on a computer screen."

"Don't worry. You're more than halfway there, and we have until this afternoon."

He rubbed his hands and grinned. "All right, now. Let's see you land this thing."

Chapter 14

Charlie

We hiked to a place called Christ's Hospital, which Emma said was about two miles away. It should have been an easy walk, but she led me down footpaths and through woodlands, so it took over an hour, and the sun was high and hot by the time we reached the ornate, brick station.

Emma bought us tickets and we sat together on a bench, holding our packs on our laps, waiting for the next train. I was unfamiliar with the railway system, but after a while I figured out that we were waiting for a train heading south, and the track on the other side was the one with trains going to London.

"What are we doing here?" I asked.

"Staying away from your friend Farber," Emma said.

"But shouldn't we be going to London?"

Emma sighed. "That's what he'll think. Once he realizes he missed you, he might go there and try to pick you up. Or he could send those men. He's not likely to think you took the southern route. And I doubt he'll be able to recruit enough helpers to cover all the trains. He'll need to concentrate on the most likely route."

I kept silent, not wanting to admit just how much use she was being. I'd have already been captured if it hadn't been for her, and I had no idea how to get to the Glastonbury Tor, especially now that we were going a different way.

A fair number of people milled about on the platform, and many of them were soldiers. There were also a few MPs, which made me nervous. I kept my eyes forward, trying to look inconspicuous, hoping that a train would come soon.

When one did come, Emma chose a carriage that was half empty. Then she took my pack and sat across the aisle from me with my pack on her lap and the other at her feet.

"What are you doing?"

"Pretending I don't know you," she said without looking at me.

"But why?"

"If you get picked up—"

"I'm not going to get picked up," I said, a little annoyed.

"But if you do," she said, "no one knows I'm with you yet. I'll be able to keep the cloak and the Talisman safe and think of a way to rescue you."

This was too much. "Rescue me? Do you know how many tight situations I've been in? And I've never needed rescuing." It was a grand boast, and not altogether true. "And besides, I've got the Talisman."

"Then give it to me," she hissed.

"What?"

"You heard me. Now, while no one is looking."

I felt like protesting, but I also felt like she might have a point, though I wasn't going to admit it. I took the Talisman out of my pocket and handed it to her. She grabbed it from my hand, looking around to make sure no one was watching, and stuffed it into a side pocket on my pack.

"Now ignore me," she said.

So, I did.

The train trundled southward, through small villages and across open land, heading for Chichester. I thought about trying to impress her by telling her I had been there before, in Roman times, but I didn't think she'd be interested. So instead, I looked out the window.

As it turned out, the train didn't go through the town of Chichester, so I couldn't look for any familiar landmarks, and when we stopped at the station, she didn't make a move to get off, so I continued to stare at the landscape. Several people got on and came to our carriage. Two of them were MPs. Young men with broad shoulders, dark hair, and pistols on their belts. They didn't look at me, but they sat in the seat directly in front of me and I felt my chest tighten.

As the train continued westward, they talked to each other and didn't seem interested in me, so I began to relax. Then one of them turned around and said, "Hell-o." I said "Hell-o" back and tried to look unconcerned.

"You RAF lads are doing a fine job," he said.

"Thanks."

"Where you heading?"

I took a quick look at my ticket. "Portsmouth."

"That's where we're going. To pick up some army bloke who went absent without leave. You?"

"Oh, I'm just, you know, going to have a look around."

"You're not based there?"

"No, I'm with the one eight eight in Horsham."

"So, a day trip then?"

"Yeah," I said. "That's right."

The guy continued to look at me and I could feel my face getting hot.

"You sound—"

"Canadian," I said.

The guy nodded. "Where's your cap?"

"I didn't want to bring it."

"That's strange. You flyboys are right proud of your uniform, especially the caps with those wings on them."

"Well, I—"

"And your uniform doesn't seem to fit you very well."

As he said it, he stood up and moved next to me, blocking the aisle. His friend stood up with him."

"Can I see your pass?"

"I … well, I …"

"You don't have one, do you?"

"Look" I said, "you can call the base, ask for Squadron Leader Fulbright. He'll vouch for me."

The man nodded. "I think we will do that." Then he grabbed my arm and pulled me upright. His friend grabbed my other arm and snapped a pair of handcuffs on me. "Until then, I think we'll keep an eye on you."

They pushed me into the seat next to the window, and one of them sat next to me. The other sat in front. We didn't talk for the rest of the journey. I just sat, my heart pounding in my chest, my cuffed hands resting in my lap, staring at the seat back in front of me, trying not to look as panicked as I felt.

It seemed an age before the train pulled into Portsmouth Harbor station. They pulled me up and marched me down the carriage and onto the platform.

Emma hadn't looked my way the whole time. And now I wasn't even sure where she was.

The station was crowded. The MPs walked me to the ticket barriers, and the guard, seeing they were MPs with a prisoner, let them through. The lobby was even more crowded, but a path opened for us, as people stepped aside and stared at me and my handcuffs.

Then I heard a scream. People stopped staring at me and looked instead to the girl carrying two packs who was shoving through the crowd.

"Soldiers," she said, rushing up to the MPs, her voice edged with panic. "They tried to assault me. They've gone that way." She pointed with the hand holding my pack. The MPs looked at each other.

"You stay with him," one of them said. "I'll check this out."

He ran into the crowd. Emma stood close, breathing hard.

"It was awful," she said, as if on the verge of tears. She held the packs by the straps, one in each hand. I saw her fists whiten.

The MP looked at her. "Why the two packs? Wait a minute. You were on the train, next to us." His hand went for his gun. "You—"

But he didn't get another word out. Emma tossed my pack to me, and I caught it in my arms as she swung the other, heavier one, up in a wide arc, smashing the MP in the face. He tumbled backward. People scattered, screaming. Emma grabbed my arm.

"Run," she said.

We barged through the crowd and into the sunshine. People shouted behind us, but we ignored them, dodging cabs and cars and horse carts as we raced across the street. There was a wide road running along the seafront. We could make good time on it, but so could the people after us.

"This way."

We turned down a side street, then she led me in a zigzag pattern, running through narrow alleys and back yards. We paused for a moment, hiding behind a low wall to catch our breath and check behind us. The sound of running feet and shouts seemed to come from all around.

"They don't know which way we went," Emma said. "They're spreading out. We need to keep moving."

She put her pack on so she could run faster. I hugged mine to my chest and ran as fast as I could.

We headed inland, where the houses got closer together and the roads narrower. Sometimes we heard running in front of us, or on the block next to us. We scurried from one alley to another, careful not to run into the people chasing us. At the end of one alley, we found a bombed-out house.

"Perfect," Emma said. "Follow me."

We vaulted over the barricades designed to keep people out and scrambled over the rubble. Inside the section of the house that was still standing, we found a ruined stairway leading to the second floor.

"Wait, that's dangerous," I said, as Emma started climbing up.

"The more dangerous the better," she said.

The stairs were tilted, and not attached to much. They groaned and creaked as she edged her way up, keeping close to the wall.

"Now you," she said, when she got to the top. "Hurry!"

I followed in her footsteps, fearing with each step that the stairs would give way beneath me. When I neared the top, Emma grabbed my arm and pulled me up.

"Now kick it."

"What?"

"Knock it down."

She sat on the floor and kicked against the top step. I sat next to her and kicked at the few bricks still holding it in place. It didn't take long. It fell with a crash and an eruption of dust. Then we sat, listening.

"What was that?" a voice from outside said.

"Over there," said another.

Emma got up and ran. "This way."

There were only two rooms on the second-floor left standing. One had no floor and only two walls, the other had three walls and half a floor. We chose that one, cramming into a corner, our backs against the rough brickwork, trying to breathe quietly.

Below us, people walked over the rubble.

"Stairs fell," a voice said. "That's all."

"Yeah, but why did they fall?" asked a second person.

"Because this whole place is about to come down, you moron. Now let's get out of here before it's all on top of our heads."

We waited, listening. Footsteps on the rubble, getting fainter. Emma put a finger to her lips. More silence. More footsteps. We kept still.

After what seemed like an hour, I pressed my lips to her ear. "What now?"

She turned her head to whisper into mine. "We wait until dark."

Chapter 15

Mitch

"Missing?" Fulbright asked.

"Yes, sir," James said.

It was five o'clock and we were in his office, right on time. We'd spent the whole day drilling and practicing, with James filling me in on all the tiny details I'd have to remember if I was going to fly the Spitfire as opposed to crashing it. We'd agreed on a story and set out with plenty of time to spare so we wouldn't be late.

Once we got to Fulbright's office, we reported that Charlie had not returned with us. He was not pleased.

"When did you last see him?"

"Just after lunch. He said he was going to have a look at the town."

"And you didn't think to report to me then?"

"He wasn't missing then, sir," James said. "He's only missing just now."

"He's AWOL now," Fulbright said, "and Farrow is going to say he's deserted. And you know what he wants to do to deserters?"

"Yes, sir."

"We had an agreement, Flight Lieutenant. You were supposed to fix this balls-up, and instead you brought me a bigger one."

"With respect," James said, "I disagree."

Fulbright folded his arms across his chest and leaned back in his chair. "I look forward to you explaining your opinion."

James cleared his throat. "Pilot Officer Hamlin was no pilot, sir."

"I could see that myself. He was barely out of training."

"No sir, I mean that literally. He wasn't a pilot. He had never flown an airplane."

Fulbright's mouth began to drop open, then he closed it, and his lips became a thin, white line.

"He wanted to come to England," James said, before Fulbright could respond. "He managed to pass himself off as a pilot and get shipped here with Kent."

Fulbright shook his head. "So, this is a compete balls-up."

"Agreed, sir. But it's not our balls-up. We were sent two men who we were told were pilots."

Fulbright started to smile, then he looked at me and frowned. "So, what about you, Pilot Officer Kent?"

"Flight Lieutenant Wyman is an excellent trainer, Sir," I said. "He has instructed me on all that is necessary to fly the Spitfire."

"That's right, sir," James cut in. "Kent is extremely knowledgeable. I am certain he will make an ace pilot. And one ace pilot is better than two mediocre pilots, or a good pilot and an impostor."

Fulbright stood. He was a tall man, muscular, and didn't look like anyone I would want to get on the wrong side of. "We'll see about that," he said. Then he looked out the window. "There's plenty of daylight left. Get your pupil aloft and see what he can do."

"Yes, sir," James said.

"And Kent," Fulbright said, glaring at me. "You damage that plane and there'll be merry hell to pay."

◆

We arrived at the hangers dressed in our sidcot suits and wearing parachutes, which made walking difficult, especially with the heavy boots I had on. In one hand I carried my leather, silk-lined gloves, in the other, my helmet. The silk scarf was already wrapped around my neck.

Two planes sat ready for us, with maintenance crews making final adjustments.

"Remember," James said, "watch what I do. Then take off and come in behind me and we'll run through a few manoeuvres."

He walked to his plane and the crew helped him onto the wing. One of the men then helped him into the cockpit, patted him on the shoulder and jumped to the ground. James gave me a thumbs up and pulled the canopy closed. He spent a few moments putting on his helmet and connecting it to the aircraft, then the engine roared to life.

Nothing in my flight simulator prepared me for that. Flames shot from the pipes and smoke billowed, filling the air with the smell of oil and exhaust. James gave a thumbs up to the crew and the plane moved forward, slewing slightly from left to right, as he had told me, so he could see where he was going.

He lined up on the runway and the engine roared louder. The plane rolled forward, faster, and faster. The tail lifted, then the wheels left the ground and the Spitfire rose into the air, over the perimeter fence and angled upward towards the sky.

My heart swelled watching it, then I remembered that I was next, and my stomach turned to ice. Then I noticed that all the other pilots had lined up along the far side of the runway. An audience, just what I didn't need.

I tried to look nonchalant as I walked towards my plane, but I was shaking all over. I had a hard time scrambling onto the wing, even with help, and the crewman who assisted me into the cockpit waited impatiently as I adjusted my seat and tried to fasten my harness. After a few failed attempts, he leaned in and helped me. Then he secured my helmet and hooked up the radio and oxygen for me. I gave him a thumbs up and tried to smile but all I could do was grimace. He patted me on the helmet, returned the thumbs up and jumped to the ground.

I checked all the dials and settings as James had instructed, and indicated to the ground crew that I was ready. Then, with equal amounts of excitement and trepidation, I started the engine. It had been startling, standing nearby when James started his engine, but sitting in the plane, it was terrifying. Flames and smoke and vibrations and a roar like I had never heard. I waited for the engine to settle, then eased the throttle forward and the plane began to roll.

As I headed out, I saw what James meant and why the slewing was necessary. The engine blocked my view, and I couldn't see anything in front of me. I turned to the left, just a little, I thought, and the plane spun in a complete circle.

I hit the brake and the plane thumped to a stop and my heart went into my throat as I thought I was going to pitch forward. I checked the temperature; it was still okay, just. But I was frozen with fear. I had no idea what to do. Across the runway, the guys were laughing and pointing, and sweat ran down my forehead. Then someone loomed over me.

It was Joe Roddis, the Chief Mechanic, a big man with sandy hair, who was in charge of the maintenance crew. I was sure he had come to drag me out of the plane, but instead he leaned into the cockpit.

"Idle it down, sir, and keep the brake on."

"Yes, sir."

"I call you sir, sir," he said. "Now, you've got to treat her gently. Easy on the steering, just a touch, and watch the brake. She's front heavy and will tip over if you try to stop too hard."

My shoulders slumped. I didn't reply, I merely nodded.

He patted my shoulder. "Don't you worry, sir," he said. "Once you get her in the air, she'll fly herself. But she's a cow on the ground, and everyone has problems on their first taxi."

I looked up at him. "My first?"

"Don't worry, sir," he said, smiling, "your secret is safe with me. But we can't have you making any more mistakes. That crew over there," he pointed across the runway, "will never let you forget it if you bottle out now. So, let me fix that dodgy back wheel for you and get you on your way."

He gave me a wink and disappeared. I leaned out the cockpit, looking for him. He was at the back of the plane, pretending to look at the rear wheel. In a few moments, he stepped away and waved to me. I gave him a thumbs up, he returned it, and I released the brake and eased forward.

This time, I turned carefully, slowly, moving left, right, left to keep an eye on where I was going. It was a relief to get to the runway. I lined up and checked the temperature. It was running hot. No time to hang about, as James had told me. I pulled the canopy closed, eased the throttle forward and the plane began to move.

I had a job keeping straight, adjusting the throttle, checking the temperature, and working the control column, as the Spitfire bounced and shuddered. The smell of hot oil and leather filled the cramped cockpit. I jostled along, the plane rattling like a bag of nails, watching the base fly by in my side vision, and the perimeter fence getting closer. I felt the plane level out as the tail rose. The engine whined, the throttle was at full power, the temperature held steady, the speed was eighty-seven miles per hour, I eased back on the control column and the jostling stopped as the Spitfire lurched into the air, taking me with it.

Chapter 16

Charlie

The afternoon lasted an age.

Sun streaked through the empty window frame and the broken wall, shining on us for the early afternoon, then leaving us in shadow just as it began to get cool. All around, the shouts and whistles of our pursuers continued. They rose and faded as the search moved from street to street. Several times the debris below clinked and rumbled as people scrambled through the ruined house for a half-hearted look.

When silence returned, and the only sounds were the normal noises from the street, Emma opened her pack and took out a canteen filled with water, cheese, and a hunk of bread. We ate and drank in silence. When we finished, she put the remaining food and water back in her pack and pulled out a blanket. We arranged it so we could sit on it, but it was only marginally more comfortable, so I took out the cloak and added that to the blanket. Then, we waited.

"We can't stay here all day," I whispered.

"We'll have to," Emma whispered back. "How far do you think we'll get with you in that uniform and your hands shackled?"

I sighed. She was right. Again.

And so, we waited some more.

I watched the sunlight move, agonizingly slow,

across the floor and walls. After an eternity, it disappeared, and the light began to fade. When twilight set in, Emma rummaged through her pack and took out a flashlight. "We need to go."

"But it's not full dark yet."

"It will be soon, and we have things to do before then."

She rose to her feet. I did the same. "Like what?"

"Getting out of here," she said.

We stowed the blanket and the cloak, and she put her pack on while I stood, cradling mine in my arms. Getting down wasn't going to be easy, especially with my hands cuffed. And in pitch blackness, it would be almost impossible.

We looked out the window. There were bushes below, but they were threaded with briers. Landing would be painful, and getting away more so. Then we peeked over the edge of the damaged floor into the darkness below. Emma put her hand over the flashlight, turned it on and allowed a single sliver of light to shine between her fingers, running it over the jagged concrete and broken bricks littering the floor below. Then she clicked it off.

"The curfew will be on now, but the wardens will be out. If they see a speck of light, they'll be on us."

There was no way we could jump down without getting injured, so we went to the hall. She flicked the flashlight again. The stairway lay below us, on its side, a wooden zigzag that would be treacherous to fall on, especially with my hands bound.

The room with no floor looked to be our best bet. The floor had landed on most of the debris so there was a relatively clean surface to land on. But it was tilted and there was no guarantee that we wouldn't break through it and hurt ourselves. Still, it was our best shot.

Emma laid our packs in the hall and held onto my hands as I slid, belly first over the edge. She struggled to hold me as my feet dangled in the air. I slipped further, almost pulling her with me, then she let go.

It wasn't a long fall. I landed on my feet but, because the floor wasn't level and I couldn't use my hands, I fell and rolled over a scattering of jagged bricks.

"Are you all right?"

My side ached and my hands were cut but I was able to get on my knees, and then my feet, balancing awkwardly on the tilted boards.

I nodded and she tossed the packs to me. The best I could do was break their fall, but they landed safely, and I scooted them out of the way. Emma wriggled over the edge as I had done. She hung briefly by her hands, then dropped, and landed next to me. The boards shifted, she fell into me, and I fell onto the bricks again.

Emma climbed off me as I moaned in pain.

"Don't you dare be hurt," she said, pulling me to my feet.

She put on her pack and headed to the nearest window. "Hurry," she said, jumping through it.

"Yeah, I'm fine, thanks," I said, following her.

Once outside, I saw the need for stealth and speed. The window we'd gone through faced the road. There was no one around, but that wouldn't last long. We raced across the lawn, climbed over the barricade, and ran, hiding behind bushes, low stone walls, and parked cars, anything to keep us from being spotted.

It was full dark now and that gave us good cover,

but it made running dangerous. We picked our way as fast as we could through the streets. There was no one around and, so far, we hadn't seen a warden.

We went up one street, turned and headed up another, zigging and zagging our way north, which I assumed was out of the city, as the ocean bordered the south and western edges. After we'd travelled a few blocks, we slipped into an alley that ran between rows of houses. These weren't the big houses we'd passed closer to the seafront. They were narrower, lower, and not as well-kept. As we worked our way along, Emma pulled herself up to look over the brick wall, shining her flashlight in short bursts, then we'd move, and she'd look again.

"This one looks good," she said at length. "Wait here."

She took off her pack, jumped up, grabbed the top of the wall, and vaulted over. I heard her moving around, then a latch clicked and a door in the wall opened. "Hurry," she said. "Leave your pack there."

I dropped my pack next to hers and ducked through the door. She closed it behind us.

We were in a long, narrow yard. Weeds grew around an assortment of rusted bikes, engine parts and scraps of metal. The house, which was really a section of a larger house, stood about a hundred feet away, visible only as a dark blot. There might have been lights on inside, but they were covered by the blackout curtains. We waited. No one came out to challenge us. Emma pulled me to the side where, tucked into the far corner of the enclosed yard, was a shed.

The door was unlocked. We slipped through, into an inky blackness that smelled of oil and grease.

Emma turned on her flashlight. A tangle of tools covered the top of a scarred workbench. At the end of the workbench was a vice.

Emma rummaged until she found a file. "This will do," she said.

She set the flashlight on the floor, so it gave us just enough light to see by. Then she had me lay the cuffs on top of the vice so she could get the file between them. She pressed the file down on the connecting chain and started sawing. After about five minutes, she'd made a small scratch in one of the links.

Then the shed lit up with dazzling light, blinding me. We both froze. I blinked.

Standing in the doorway was a man, short and skinny, with greasy black hair. He wore a stained undershirt with no sleeves, baggy pants, and a flat cap. One hand was on the light switch, the other held a knife.

"Well, well," he said, "look what we have here."

Chapter 17

Mitch

The Spitfire practically flew itself, and was better in every way than the biplane I had flown in 1916: more comfortable, more powerful, faster, and so responsive it seemed to know where I wanted to go before I did. I reached down for the landing gear lever and pumped the wheels up. The speed increased. I climbed to where James was and caught up with him.

The radio crackled in my ear. "Let's take you through your paces now," James said.

He led me through some tight turns, left and right and up and down. We zoomed this way and that, at incredible speed. I followed him up at an almost vertical angle, then we dived straight down. When we reached the coast, we did long, looping curves, rising higher and higher. At twenty-thousand feet he came beside me.

"We're going to stall now," James said over the radio. "Throttle back. At about eighty, it should start to fall. Don't panic; just do what I say."

I cut the speed. The plane slowed. For a while, it seemed to hover in the air. All around me was blue sky. It was magnificent. I felt like the king of the world. Then the plane fell out of the sky.

Suddenly, I was pointing straight down, spinning and plummeting towards the Channel. I tried to see if

James was beside me, but everything was spinning so fast. And yet, I wasn't scared. I knew what a stall felt like, I just needed to figure out how to get a Spitfire out of one. James issued instructions even as his plane plummeted along with mine, but I barely heard him. I jostled the stick and worked the rudder and flaps, stopping the spin, then I pulled the plane level. It was travelling at an amazing speed, so I climbed to slow it down.

When I levelled out, James came up beside me.

"You didn't follow any of my instructions," he said. I waited for the chewing out, but then he said, "yet you pulled out of that like you've been flying all your life. Well done."

I smiled and felt my heart swell. We did a few more manoeuvres, then headed back inland. I watched the ground, picking out landmarks. Near the base, we flew in widening circles, allowing me to study the land below, making notes in my memory.

The sun was going down, yet it felt as if we'd been up for only a few minutes. And I felt like I wanted to stay up forever. But the radio crackled again, and James said, "I'm going to land now. Watch me. Then come in yourself."

I climbed and flew in tight circles, keeping an eye on the other Spitfire. James lined up and I followed above him, watching as he descended towards the base. He cleared the perimeter fence, then dropped to the ground. I flew overhead as his plane came to a halt and saw his hand wave through the canopy as he opened it.

I dipped my wings and flew on, making a wide turn. As I came back over the base, I saw the other pilots lining up along the runway, coming out to see me screw up my landing. The last thing I wanted was an audience, but I wasn't going to give them the show they wanted. I'd give them another show, instead.

I flew over the base, low, doing barrel rolls, then I pulled the plane up and did a loop the loop, screaming down towards the base before levelling out and streaking away to a distance where I could begin my landing run.

I throttled back, trying to lose speed. Once I spied the base, I pumped the wheels down until they locked and the light went green. Then I lined up. One-hundred and eighty. I throttled back more. At one-forty I put the flaps down. The nose came up and I had to throttle up to level out. It was difficult because I couldn't see in front of me. I just had to hope I was still on course. The hedges flew by beneath me. Eighty-eight miles an hour. I angled in, cutting the power. The perimeter fence, then grass beneath me. I cut more speed and felt a thump as the wheels hit the ground. The plane bumped and rattled, and I struggled to hold it straight. I throttled back and resisted the urge to step on the brake. The plane rumbled to a stop, and I let out a breath I hadn't been aware I was holding.

I taxied back to the hanger, where James stood by his plane, waiting. The crew came out to meet me. I rolled up, cut the engine, and pulled back the canopy. One of the crew helped me out of the harness and onto the wing. I jumped to the ground and found myself face to face with Fulbright.

I stood to attention, my parachute hanging off my back and my helmet under my arm.

"If you buzz my base like that again I'll have your guts for garters," he said.

I felt my face go hot. My mouth opened but no sound came out. Then Fulbright smiled.

"But that was some flying. You're quite the ace, aren't you?"

Then James was beside me, slapping me on the back. Fulbright turned to him. "You did a great job, Red. We might be down one pilot, but the one we got is certainly worth his salt."

Chapter 18

Charlie

Emma dropped the file and grabbed a claw hammer off the workbench. The man put his free hand up, palm out.

"Easy now, young lady," he said.

Emma raised the hammer. The man folded his knife, put it in his pocket, and took a step forward. "You're the ones they're looking for, aren't you?"

Emma said nothing. She raised the hammer higher.

"Don't fret," the man said. "I'm no grass. All I want is for you to not ruin a perfectly good set of handcuffs."

"A grass?" I asked.

"He means he won't turn us in," Emma said. She looked at me. "Do you think we can trust him?"

I shrugged. "Do we have a choice?"

"Now you're talking sense," the man said. "Put that hammer down. I'll get those handcuffs off if you let me keep them. Deal?"

Emma lowered the hammer but kept it in her hand. "All right. But you leave the knife down there. Deal?"

The man smiled, showing tobacco-stained teeth. "That's one cagey bird you've got there, son," he said, taking the knife out of his pocket. He laid it, unopened, on the far end of the bench and came towards us.

Emma stepped aside. The man lifted my hands and studied the handcuffs. "Quality item, these. Worth a bob or two."

He picked up a tool from the workbench. It looked like a small knife, but when he opened it, there were no blades, just a few oddly shaped wires. He stuck one of the wires into the keyhole, twisted it a few times and the handcuff opened. Then he did the other one. I rubbed my wrists, glad to finally be free.

"Thanks, Mister," Emma said, laying the hammer down. "We'll be on our way now."

"Sure thing," the man said, walking towards the door. Then he turned back to us, the knife in his hand. The blade snapped open, glinting in the harsh light. "As soon as you give me all your money."

Emma stepped close to me. I gaped at the man, who was still smiling. "I thought you weren't a grass."

The man chuckled and shook his head. "I'm not, but I am a thief. Money now. And don't get any cute ideas about picking up that hammer again."

The man came close, within striking distance, but there was no way we could jump him without getting stabbed. Emma must have thought the same thing. Her shoulders slumped and she sighed. "All right."

She dug in her pocket and pulled out the few bills she had left. The man snatched the money out of her hand and stuffed it in his pocket.

"That was very civilized. I'll let you go now."

I felt like we had gotten off lightly, and I was ready to go, but Emma stood her ground.

"Wait," she said. "You've got to leave us some money. We need bus fare."

The man smirked. "Sounds like you have a problem."

"We'll make a deal."

The man looked at his knife. "You're not in a position—"

"Yes, we are. As soon as we get away from you, we'll find a cop. You might not be a grass," she said, gazing straight at the man, "but I am." She motioned to me. "He'll get a few weeks in a military prison, and I'll likely be let off. But how much time do you think you'll be serving for misappropriating military equipment? And there was an interesting assortment of scrap metal in your garden."

I clamped my mouth shut so it wouldn't fall open and tried to keep the shocked look off my face.

The man shook his head. "And why do you think you'll get a chance to do that?"

"Because you might be a thief," Emma said, "but you're no murderer."

The man looked dumbfounded, then he started to laugh. "That's some bird you've got there," he said to me, "I'd keep her if I was you."

"She's not my girlfriend," I said. "She's my cousin."

"Sure," the man said, "if you like. Now tell me, what's your deal."

"An RAF uniform," Emma said. "Give us some money back and you can have it."

The man laughed again. "How about I just take it?"

"I'd like to see you try," I said.

The man looked at Emma, then at me. I stood straight and puffed out my chest.

"It's bound to come in handy," Emma said,

"considering the business you're in. You'll make your money back and then some."

"Your … cousin," the man said, smiling, "has quite the sharp mind."

He folded the knife and put it in his pocket. "Okay, let's do business. Take it off."

"Money first," Emma said.

"My, she drives a hard bargain," he said, looking at me again. "Do you always let her do your talking for you?"

"She talks," I said, "I take action."

He laughed again. "The entertainment alone is worth the price." He took our money from his pocket, pulled off a single bill and handed it to me.

"Not enough," Emma said.

He shook his head. "No cap. That takes a bit off the price. Now get it off."

I looked at Emma. She nodded and I undressed, thinking I had made a good choice in exchanging my tighty-whities for the 1940s version of underwear. The bottoms were longer than boxer shorts and clung to my thighs like white cycling shorts, and I had an undershirt, equally tight, that could pass for a white tee shirt. My socks were just blue socks, but at least they were thick.

While I undressed, Emma picked up her flashlight and put it in her pocket. I was afraid the man would steal that too, but he took no notice. When I finished, I handed the bundle over. He took it and stepped aside.

"Pleasure doing business with you."

We squeezed by, still wary of him. "If I were you," he said to me, "I'd steal some clothes as soon as you can."

Emma ran out the door. And I ran after her.

Back in the alley, Emma stowed her flashlight, took the money from me and we put on our packs.

"What on earth were you thinking?" I asked as we jogged back down the alley.

"We needed the money," she said, "and that uniform was a liability. We were going to have to ditch it anyway. You stuck out like a sore thumb."

I ran my hand down my front, from my chest to my knees. "And I don't stick out in this?"

We reached the road and began running north.

"Well, I didn't see you coming up with any bright ideas," she said.

"Arguing with a criminal isn't exactly smart."

We turned down another road. My feet began to ache from the stones on the pavement.

"What? Now I'm stupid? How far do you think you would have gone without me?"

"I've done pretty well before, without anyone selling my clothes right off me."

"So, you want to go it alone? Is that what you want?"

"I want—"

I wasn't sure what I wanted, and I didn't get a chance to find out, because the shrill blast of a whistle cut through the night, followed by someone shouting.

"You two, stop!"

Chapter 19

Mitch

After we stowed our gear and had a bath, and changed into fresh uniforms, James took me to the Officers' Mess. We ate by ourselves, as dinnertime had already come and gone. None of the people waiting on us complained, however. In fact, they were cheery, and called us both "Sir," which I found a little odd at first.

Leaving the mess, it was full dark. There were lights around the base, but it wasn't lit up the way a modern camp would be, so I could still see the stars. James led the way down a gravel path to the Officers' Club. I felt tired and peaceful, soothed by the rhythmic crunching of the gravel under our feet, breathing the cool night air with its scent of grass mixed with a lingering whiff of exhaust.

Then we reached the Club. James opened the door and any peace I felt was shattered as harsh light, billows of tobacco smoke, and a jumble of competing sounds tumbled out. I followed James inside and he shut the door, sealing us into the smoky, chaotic room.

It was large, and square, with an assortment of tables scattered around the floor. The pilots sat at the tables, talking to each other, and shouting between tables. Somewhere, music played, but it was nearly drowned out by the raucous laughter and harsh voices.

James led me across the room to the bar. He leaned up against it, so I did too. Then he took a large glass from the bartender and handed it to me. It was filled to the brim with warm, flat beer. He took one for himself, clinked it against mine—spilling both our drinks—and raised it up. "To a successful run."

I raised my glass, then followed his lead by taking a big gulp from it. It tasted awful. Worse, even, than the small beer we'd had to drink in the Middle Ages. I tried not to grimace.

James laughed. "Not used to real beer where you come from?"

"It's different, is all," I said, choking down another mouthful.

Two pilots came to the bar, their caps at different angles, their ties loose and their shirts partly unbuttoned. They slammed empty glasses on the bar. "Hey, Red, still babysitting the Canuck?"

James nodded. "Hey, Yo-Yo, Ziggy. We're just back from a re-con flight. Can't have our new pilot getting lost."

"That can't be easy," the one called Ziggy said. "Heard he doesn't know which way to go."

The other pilot laughed. "Spun around in a circle, he did."

James smiled. "Come on, fellas, that was a mechanical failure. Kent knows what he's doing."

The bartender handed full glasses to them. They laughed again and turned to head back to their table. "Sure he does. Wrong-way Kent knows exactly which way to go."

This made them laugh harder, and they struggled

to keep their beer from spilling as they doubled over and staggered to their chairs. My stomach went cold, and I suddenly felt sick.

"Drink up," James said, "I'll get you another."

I looked at the pilots, huddled together, laughing and joking. "I don't know."

"Don't let it bother you," James said. "Now finish your pint. Your ability to hold your beer is also being assessed."

I took another gulp, and another. At last, the glass was empty. James immediately replaced it with a full one.

"Cheers," he said, clinking my glass again.

I sighed and took a sip, surprised that it didn't taste as bad. So, I took another. "How long do I have to be here before I'm accepted," I asked without meaning to.

James laughed. "How long? You just got here this morning. Give it some time."

Suddenly, I felt strangely maudlin. I turned to James and leaned towards him. "I've fought with knights, I was in the Battle of Hastings, I was at Tilbury, I flew a Night Fighter in World War One, but I've never had so much trouble fitting in. And I've never wanted to fit in as badly."

James put a hand on my shoulder. "Hey, it's all right. You're doing fine, trust me. Let me get you another drink."

To my surprise, my glass was empty. A fresh one appeared in my hand.

"You still have a lot more to learn," James said. "We'll go back up tomorrow. And the day after. They'll see what you can do. They'll—"

A hand appeared on James's shoulder. "Why don't

you join your mates, Red," Fulbright said. "Mr. Kent and I need to talk."

James nodded and strolled off. The pilots greeted him with shouts and back slapping as he settled at the table. "Wishing you were part of the group?" Fulbright asked.

He was holding a whisky glass. His hat was on straight, his shirt buttoned. "Well, yeah," I said, "Sir."

"No need for that here," Fulbright said.

I took another sip of beer. It tasted good. "Yes, sir."

Fulbright kept silent for a few moments, then he pointed at the pilots with the hand holding the whisky glass, and said, "Those boys, those men, they have more flight hours under their belts than you can dream of. Every one of them has flown combat missions. Many have exchanged fire with the enemy, and a few have kills. I was impressed with your flying because I know that was your first time in a Spitfire. But to them, you were just showing off. And no one likes a show off."

"Yes, sir."

"You have a way to go before anyone here is going to be impressed with you." He stopped and took a sip of his whisky.

"I have never before wanted so badly to be part of a unit," I said, surprising myself.

Fulbright smiled. "You and every other hotshot pilot. But don't worry, you're on your way. I think the best thing for you now, however, is to get a good night's sleep."

I nodded. My glass was empty again and I had been about to ask for another.

"I want you up at first light. Red will take you out

115

again, show you battle formations and how to shoot. Keep an eye on the landscape. In the afternoon, you're going out solo."

My heart started to pound. "Yes, sir."

"So, I'm ordering you to barracks. Get some kip. And be up on time."

I thanked him and the bartender, and waved to James on my way out, but he was too involved with a conversation to notice.

The door closed behind me, blocking out the light and noise and smoke. I made my way towards the barracks, feeling thrilled and terrified in equal measure, and thinking that this would be a bad time to run into the real Johnny Kent. Or Farber.

Thinking of Farber made me wonder how Charlie was doing.

Chapter 20

Charlie

"Warden," Emma said. "This way."

We ran down the street and cut into an alley, but footsteps followed us. It was so dark we couldn't see him. We could only hear him.

"Stop."

A flashlight beam lit up the alley, bouncing as the warden raced after us. It proved to be an advantage, however, because now we could see, and we ran even faster.

At the end of the alley, we cut across some front lawns, vaulting the low brick walls. Then the warden came out of the alley. He was unsure which way we had gone, but then he spotted us and shouted for us to stop again.

We ran down the middle of the road. It exposed us, but it was easier to run there. Unfortunately, it was easier for the warden too. We turned down a side street, and then into another alley, and the warden followed.

Emma took a quick look behind us. "How is he tracking us? It's pitch dark."

"I stand out like a beacon," I said. "I might as well be carrying glow sticks."

"Glow what?"

"Never mind. We need to get out of sight."

At the end of the alley, we hit another street. We ran as fast as we could, trying to get as far away from the alley as we could before the warden emerged.

We were pretty far away, but he picked us up immediately.

"I need to hide all this white," I said.

"How?"

"I don't know."

I thought about wrapping myself in the cloak, but there wasn't time. We turned down a side street. Before we got to the end, the warden picked us up again.

"Stop."

The street ended. There was nothing else there, no houses, just a blank space. I was afraid we had come to the ocean but there were darker clumps spaced around the black expanse.

"It's a park," I said. "This way. I have an idea."

We raced towards the nearest dark cluster. It was a stand of trees.

"Pack off. Lay down," I said.

"What?"

"Just do it."

I threw my own pack on the ground, ripped it open, and pulled out the cloak.

"Down, now," I said, as I unfurled it.

She laid on the ground, next to her pack. I laid down beside her and covered us with the cloak.

"What are you doing?"

"Hiding," I said, keeping my voice low.

"But he'll see—"

"No, he won't. He'll be looking for someone standing up dressed in white. The cloak is dark. It will blend in with the ground. Unless he steps on us, he won't find us. As long as we keep quiet."

Footsteps came close, then stopped.

"I know you're in there. Come out."

A flash of light passed over us as he scanned the park. But the footsteps came no closer.

"Bloody yobs," the warden said. His footsteps receded. Silence.

"Is he gone?" Emma asked.

"I don't know," I said, "but keep still. As long as we're under here it's like we're covered with Harry Potter's cloak of invisibility."

"Who's what?"

"Never mind. Just keep quiet."

We waited. No sound came.

The ground was soft, covered with leaves and grass, but it was cold. I felt my joints getting stiff.

"We should go," I said.

"Go where?"

"To wherever you were taking us in the first place."

"That was to the bus station, but they're closed now, and we need to get you some clothes first."

"Then we need to go find me some clothes."

Emma shook her head. "If we go back into town, another warden will surely see us. If we're invisible here, this is where we need to stay."

"But what about my clothes?"

"Leave that to me."

"What, you're in charge of this expedition suddenly?"

"Pardon me for having good ideas."

"And here I am, half naked and freezing to death. Great idea."

She threw the cloak aside and stood up. I thought

she was going to stalk off in a huff, but instead she took off her shirt.

"Here," she said, holding it out to me, "lay on this."

"But—"

"Just do it."

"You don't have to be a martyr for my sake."

She threw the shirt at me and started undoing her pants.

"I'm not being a martyr," she hissed. "I'm trying to save your life. If you lay on the ground like that all night, you'll die of hypothermia. If we're going to stay here, I'd prefer you alive in the morning."

She kicked off her shoes and danced on one leg, then the other, to get her pants off. Her underwear looked a lot like mine, just as white and covering just as much.

I laid her shirt out as a ground cloth, like they taught us in Boy Scouts, while Emma wrestled with her pants. "Get down. You'll be seen."

She laid out her pants, shoved my pack at me and took her own, pulling out the blanket. She laid it over her pants and shirt, giving us a softer, warmer bed. Then she laid down, using her pack as a pillow.

"There," she said, pulling the cloak back over us. "We'll both be equally cold. Or warm."

"Look," I said, "you don't have to—"

"I'm sorry if I bruised your ego by having some good ideas," she said. "I just want to help. I don't think you're incompetent. Annie told me about the brave things you did, but she also told me how she helped you. She made a difference, and I want my chance to make a difference. Pulling up potatoes is all well and good, but I want to be more than just a Land

Girl. I thought you'd welcome my help, but you don't seem to see anything in me except a meddling child."

She rolled on her side and started to shudder. I laid on my back, the cloak over my face, staring at the darkness. She couldn't know the reason I didn't want her to come. I felt frustrated and helpless. The truth was, I wouldn't have even gotten out of town without her help, and that infuriated me, but not for the reason she thought.

Her breathing eased. I shuffled onto my side, facing her back, close but not touching. I couldn't see her, but I smelled her hair, smelled her.

"I think," I whispered, "that you are the bravest girl I have ever met."

She said nothing, but reached around and took my hand, pulling my arm around her and cradling it to her chest. I moved closer and she melted into me, giving me her warmth, and taking mine.

I sighed and fell asleep.

Chapter 21

Mitch

"C'mon, Kent. Time to fly."

I opened my eyes. It was still dark. My mouth felt dry, and my head thumped with a dull but persistent throbbing. James looked in better shape than I felt, and he had come in much later than I did.

I groaned and climbed out of bed.

Once again, we ate alone in the mess hall, waited on by bleary-eyed servers. Then James led me to my airplane. By the time we had suited up, it was beginning to get light. The mechanics were already at work, checking the Spitfires and testing their engines, filling the air with the smell of exhaust. The noise shattered the peaceful dawn and made my head throb harder.

"Formation flying today," James said, climbing into his aircraft. "Line up with me on the runway. We'll take off together. Stick to my starboard side, just behind me."

The mechanics helped me into the cockpit. I hooked the radio and oxygen to my helmet and put it on, breathing deep to clear my thinking. I did my checks, started the engine, and waited for the smoke to clear. The plane vibrated and the roar of the propeller was deafening. James taxied away. I followed.

He lined up on the runway and I moved my plane as close to him as I dared. At least I didn't have an audience this time, hoping that I'd screw up. The runway sparkled with dew under the first rays of the morning sun. Up in the sky a few clouds drifted by. It looked peaceful, which was more than I could say for how I felt.

James's Spitfire roared louder and lurched forward. I pushed the throttle and felt my plane move. This was harder than taking off alone. I had to keep checking the gauges, the steering, the throttle, and make sure I didn't run into James. The Spitfire rattled and bounced, and I struggled to keep a safe distance. The roar, the clatter, the bouncing, and I found I couldn't do anything except keep an eye on James's plane and trust he was at take-off speed. I watched his tail rise, then felt mine do the same. Light showed under his wheels and my plane bounced into the air. I wanted to breathe a sigh of relief but found I could do nothing but follow and hope.

We cleared the perimeter. I pumped up the landing gear and followed James into the air.

Flying formation wasn't as hard as I thought it would be. I tucked up behind James as he instructed and then just had to keep him in my sight. The Spitfire flew like a dream, so even as we climbed and turned and descended, all I had to do was keep him in my peripheral vision. Soon, I found I was able to enjoy myself, gazing around at the open, blue sky and the wisps of clouds, and the rolling green of Sussex below.

We climbed to twenty-thousand feet and flew straight and fast towards the coast. When the green gave way to grey water, James told me it was time to test my cannons.

The radio crackled in my ear. "Dive for the deck. Use your sight to pick a spot and, when you get close, press the fire button. Remember what I told you. And be careful to not crash into the ocean."

"On my way," I said.

I nosed the Spitfire into a dive, gaining speed as I descended. I watched the water coming at me through the sight—an angled square of glass with a crosshair projected onto it—and imagined an enemy plane. Then I squeezed the trigger.

I held it for only a second. The Spitfire, James had told me, could fire 1,150 rounds per minute, giving me only fifteen seconds of firing time. Holding the trigger down would not only overheat my cannons, it would use up all my ammo in one go. A second or two was plenty.

The boom of the guns pounded in my ears, and the plane shook as spirals of smoke from the tracer bullets screamed downward. The ocean rushed up to meet me and the smell of gunpowder mingled with the scent of oil and leather. Bullets strafed the rippling ocean, sending geysers into the air. The speed and pounding were so great they mesmerized me. I shook my head and pulled back on the stick. The Spitfire levelled out. I pulled back further and shot into the air.

I took a few breaths to calm myself, and realized I was hot and sweaty and buzzing with adrenaline.

"Not too bad," James said. "Try it again, but don't go so low this time. I thought we were going to have to send a boat to fish you out of the Channel."

I dived again, with more control this time, concentrating on keeping the bullets hitting the same spot. After a few more runs, James seemed satisfied.

"That was good practice," he said. "You can shoot a stationery target, but remember, in a dogfight you'll be shooting at moving targets that will be shooting back at you. Keep your wits about you."

"Yes, sir," I said, settling in behind him.

"And remember this. We will fly in formation, straight and level, to the battle. But once in the battle, never fly straight and level for more than ten seconds. If you do, someone will get a bead on you, and by twelve seconds, your plane will be full of holes."

"I'll remember that."

"You will, or you'll end up at the bottom of the Channel. Now, do a few more."

I spent the next half hour practicing diving, climbing, and turning, imagining an enemy plane, and trying to shoot where I thought it would be. When the ammunition ran out, we formed up and headed back to base.

My hands throbbed from the vibrations and the cockpit was stifling but I had never felt better. The clouds zipped by, and the quilted countryside below rolled on and on. It was breathtaking. At that moment, I wanted nothing more than to be an RAF pilot and I felt a wrenching in my chest when I thought that this was not a place I could stay. The real Johnny Kent was sure to show up soon. My only hope was that Charlie could finish his mission and somehow get back to me before that happened. But in my heart, I wished that Kent might remain missing, and that Charlie would finish his task and return home without me. If that happened, I wouldn't mind a bit.

The radio crackled, startling me. "Coming up

now," James said. "Make your landing. I'll follow you in."

I circled around the base, watching for landmarks. It all looked familiar now. I lined up, did my checks and, after lowering the landing gear, sailed in for a bumpy landing with James right behind. Then we taxied to the hangers where the crew helped me out.

James greeted me on the ground with a slap on the back. "You're doing great, Mitch … I mean, Kent. Just one more test and you'll be at the level Fulbright expects."

I nodded. "What test."

"After lunch, you'll do a solo flight. Around the Isle of White and back."

We walked together towards the barracks. "That's it?"

"Sure. All you need to do is not get lost."

I nodded, but suddenly didn't feel so good.

Chapter 22

Charlie

I woke to someone pulling at me. I sat up quickly, ready to fight or run, and saw Emma tugging at the shirt I was lying on. It was grey dawn and chilly. My head swam from sitting up so quickly.

"What are you doing?"

Emma stood over me, dressed in her pants and heavy shoes, with her cap pulled low over her ears.

"I'm going into town," she said, putting the shirt on. "We need supplies."

"You can't. It's too dangerous."

"They're looking for an RAF pilot accompanied by a girl," she said, fastening the buttons. "A girl on her own won't attract attention." She tucked the shirt in. "Now lay back down and keep quiet. I won't be long."

There was no point arguing with her, so I laid back on the blanket. It was colder now, without the shirt and pants under it, and Emma next to me. I pulled the cloak up and Emma covered my head.

"I'm going to camouflage you a bit," she said, "so the cloak won't be so visible."

There came the sound of leaves and dirt hitting the cloak, then she walked away.

I laid still, listening. Soon, the birds began to sing. Occasionally, a car or truck chugged past on the

127

nearby road, or the sound of horse hooves clopping on pavement and the creaking of wheels told me a cart was going by. Even from beneath the cloak I could see it was getting lighter. I wondered how long I would have to lay there, and what I would do if she didn't come back. I didn't want to admit it, but I needed her. There was no way I could get to the Tor without her. Yet it pained me to think what might happen then.

After what seemed an eternity, I heard footsteps approaching. The cloak lifted and Emma looked down at me. She held a bundle of clothes under one arm, and in her other hand—the one holding the edge of the cloak—was a paper bag.

"Put these on," she said, dropping the clothes on me.

I sat up and put on the shirt. It was heavy flannel, worn but comfortable, and warm. Emma, I noticed, no longer had her Land Girl clothes on. Instead, she had black leather shoes with flat soles, a brown skirt that hung to her knees, and a light blue blouse. Over the blouse, she wore a darker blue, corduroy jacket. Her hat was gone, and her red hair hung free, falling over her shoulders.

"Like it?" she asked when she saw me looking. She did a twirl, making her skirt billow out and her hair lash across her face.

Her clothes, as well as mine, were old and faded, but that would be an advantage. New clothes would make us stand out.

"You look great," I said. "Did you steal them?"

"No," she said, "I got them from a rag and bone man." She ran her free hand down her front. "I traded my old clothes for them."

I stood to put on the pants. They were denim and came with a set of suspenders. Awkwardly, I attempted to put them on.

Emma laughed. She put the paper bag on the cloak and helped me. "Don't you wear braces where you come from?"

"You mean, suspenders?"

She laughed again, harder this time. "I hope you don't wear suspenders."

I shrugged, confused, but I was getting used to it. I sat and put on the shoes, a sturdy pair of leather work boots, but not too heavy. Good for running. The final piece of clothing was a flat cap. I put it on, then Emma adjusted it.

"There," she said, "now you fit in."

We sat side by side on the cloak. Emma took two buttered rolls out of the bag and handed me one. It was still warm and tasted divine.

We ate the rolls in silence and drank the last of the water in the canteen.

"I bought two sandwiches for lunch," she said, putting the bag and the empty canteen into her pack. "We'll need to fill that soon. But right now, we need to get going."

"To where?"

"To catch a bus."

I stowed the cloak and checked that the Talisman was still safe, then we put on our packs and walked deeper into the park. We strolled through grass until it ended, then rejoined the road. There were few people out, and none of them paid us any attention.

"When we're around people," Emma said, looking around to make sure we were alone, "keep quiet."

"What for?"

"Your accent," she said. "It's a dead giveaway."

"Well, maybe I can try to talk like you."

I made an attempt, but it got her laughing.

"Sorry," she said, "not convincing. You'll be better off pretending you're mute. If anyone does talk to you, just shake your head."

We walked on, going up one street and then another. The houses thinned out, and more green land appeared. The sun rose and cars and trucks became more plentiful. More than a few, I noted, were military vehicles. I tried not to notice them and kept walking.

We passed a pub. It was closed, but there was an outdoor spigot. Emma filled her canteen and we continued on our way.

At length, we came to a wooden bus shelter where a line of people waited. We joined them.

"Can we get a bus to Salisbury from here?" Emma asked the woman in front of her.

"Be here in about ten minutes," the woman said without turning. "If they're on schedule."

"A miracle if they are," the woman ahead of her said. Others in the line chuckled, then settled back into silence.

Ten minutes passed, then ten more. After half an hour, a double-decker bus with a green roof and cream-colored sides rumbled up. A few people got off. The women shuffled forward, past the driver, who was sealed in his own compartment. We followed. Emma pulled me up the stairs. The bus lurched forward, almost making me lose my balance.

"Don't we have to pay?" I asked.

She held a finger to her lips and continued pulling me down the aisle.

The upper deck was nearly empty. There were only a few people up there with us, and they were all sitting near the big window in the front, smoking cigarettes. We took the bench seat in the back near a window with the sign "Emergency Exit" over it and a hammer-shaped piece of metal on a chain dangling next to it.

Soon, a man in a blue uniform and cap trudged up the steps. "New fares!"

Emma took the bill out of her pocket. The man came to her. "Two singles to Salisbury," she said.

The man put the bill in a pouch hanging from his belt. Then punched out a ticket on a machine he was carrying and counted out a few copper coins from another device on his belt.

"You two travelling together?" he asked.

Emma nodded. "Yes."

"Did you come from Portsmouth?"

"No. We got on in Cosham."

The man looked at me. "I know that. But were you in Portsmouth last night?"

"No," Emma said. "We were in Cosham, visiting our mum. We're going home now."

"You live in Salisbury, then?"

Emma nodded.

"You're a bit young," the man said still looking at me. "Strange you're living on your own."

"There's a war on," Emma said. "Lots of strange things are happening."

The man continued looking at me. "Does your boyfriend talk?"

Emma leaned forward. "That's my brother," she said, keeping her voice low. "He's a bit simple."

The man glowered at me. "He's not going to be

any trouble, is he?"

"No, he just doesn't talk much."

The man's eyes narrowed, but he turned and walked back down the aisle.

"I little simple," I said, when he had gone downstairs.

"Better than having you talk. I think he's suspicious. They probably told people to keep an eye out for us."

I nodded. "Why are we going to Salisbury?"

"Because that's as far as our money will take us."

"What are we going to do when we get there?"

Emma took off her pack and set it beside her.

"We'll worry about that when the time comes. Now keep quiet and try to look stupid."

Chapter 23

Mitch

Flight one, the Blue and Green sections, had been scrambled to hunt down a reconnaissance flight so there were only a few of us at lunch, but that was enough. They kidded James about babysitting "the Canuck" and didn't say a word to me. When he told them I was going to solo out to Salisbury, one of them said I'd probably end up in Dover and they all laughed.

I leaned close to ask James why that was so funny, and he told me it was in the opposite direction. I pushed my plate away, having lost my appetite.

After lunch we went to the barracks where James went through the trip with me. I was to fly to the Isle of Wight, then on to Bournemouth and up to Salisbury. After that, I was to set a course for Brighton, then find my way back to the base using just landmarks.

"The main thing," he said, "is to keep your bearings. If you get lost, the worst thing you can do is fly around trying to find out where you are, run out of petrol and crash."

I took a breath, trying to calm my nerves. "Has that ever happened."

James nodded. "Not in this squadron, but some new pilots have come a cropper that way."

He saw the look on my face and clapped his hand on my shoulder. "Don't worry. Just keep your wits about you. You'll do fine."

I still wasn't convinced, and James must have seen it because he looked around to make sure no one was nearby and said, "The men think you're just going up to get the lay of the land, and you are, but this is your final test. If you can navigate through this course, Fulbright will accept you as a full member of the squadron."

I nodded but said nothing.

"Look, all you have to do is make it back. It's two hundred miles. If all goes well, you'll be back in less than three hours."

I nodded again, thinking about being a member of the squadron with the nickname Wrongway.

We walked to the hanger, where my plane was fuelled, rearmed and ready. I suited up, put on my parachute and life jacket, and the crew helped me into the cockpit.

I was nervous taking off, sure the guys were watching me, but once in the air the familiar thrill overtook me, and I forgot all about them. I climbed to twenty-thousand feet, set my course for the Isle of Wight, and enjoyed the feeling of zooming through the air with nothing, and no one, around to bother me. James had given me an easy test. If I managed to miss the Isle of Wight, then I didn't deserve to be in the squadron. I settled down and concentrated on keeping the plane pointed in the right direction.

I wasn't dead centre on the Isle of Wight, but I did hit it. I cruised past, circled around, and flew over again, this time in the centre. From there, Bournemouth was easy; it took about five minutes.

The course to Salisbury was my first tricky one. I could easily miss a small city if I wasn't careful. I turned to the correct heading and concentrated on keeping on course and correcting for drift. After a tense fifteen minutes, the city came up just as expected, though I was a little to the port side of it. I corrected and turned onto my last leg for Brighton. After that, it would be easy.

Green fields and woodlands eased by below me. I realized I was as close to the Glastonbury Tor as I was likely to get and wondered if Charlie had made it yet. For some reason, I had the feeling he hadn't. Not yet. He might be somewhere below, still trying to get there. I hoped he wasn't having too hard a time.

I put it out of my mind and concentrated on enjoying the freedom of flight. Soon, I was over the South Downs and realized I was nearing Brighton. In a short time, I would be back on the ground, a fully-fledged member of the one eight eight Squadron.

That thought brought mixed feelings, so I didn't think about it. Instead, I watched the stunning countryside, listened to the roar of the engine, and breathed in the scents of leather and oil, which instilled such joy that I couldn't be concerned what the others thought of me. I was an RAF pilot, guiding a Spitfire through the sky and there was nothing else like it in the world.

Then I saw the German bomber, and its two Messerschmitt escorts.

Chapter 24

Charlie

The bus rumbled through the countryside on narrow roads, stopping at towns with names like Southwick, Wickham and Curdridge. Sometimes, a bell rang, and the bus would stop, seemingly in the middle of nowhere, and a person or two would get off. Other times, a person standing on the side of the road would put out their hand and the bus would pull over to let them on.

Some people came to the top deck, but none sat near us. The man in the blue uniform, who Emma told me was the conductor, would then come up with his call of, "New fares."

It was all strange to me. Aside from the school bus, I had never ridden in a bus back home, and I wondered how much different it would be. I was pretty sure there wouldn't be a hammer hanging next to a window that you were supposed to bash out if you got into trouble.

We meandered on through back lanes. As noon approached, we ate our sandwiches and sipped from the water bottle. At a town called Eastleigh, the driver announced he was making a comfort stop. He and the conductor talked for a minute outside the bus, then they both went down the street.

Emma watched them go, a concerned look on her

face.

"I don't like this," she said.

"Why not?"

"That conductor. He seemed suspicious. He might be up to something."

"Like what?"

She shrugged. "I don't know. But if he is, it won't be good for us."

"Do you think we should get off here?"

"I don't know," she said, looking up and down the street. It was a bigger town than some of the others, but still fairly small. "There might not be another bus for a while."

We weighed the pros and cons but before we could decide, the driver came back, and then the conductor, and it was too late. The engine rumbled and the bus jerked forward, taking us with it.

She sat up straight, keeping an eye on the road. We travelled down more country lanes and through more small towns, picking up people and dropping others off. After a while we began to relax. Then, after we passed through a little town called West Grimstead, the bus pulled to the side of the road.

There was no reason to stop. The bell hadn't rung and there was no one waiting to get on. In fact, there didn't seem to be anyone around.

All we could see was a large, black car parked on the road in front of the bus.

Standing next to the car was Farber.

"We have to get out of here," Emma said.

She grabbed her pack. I put mine on and we started down the aisle. I heard footsteps on the stairs and the conductor appeared.

"You said he wouldn't be any trouble" he barked.

"Now come with me. A man outside wants to see you."

We tried to backtrack, but he grabbed Emma. I put my arms around her and pulled while he yanked on her arm. I was losing the tug-o-war, so I pushed forward. The conductor fell back, with Emma on top of him and me on top of her.

"C'mon," I said.

We jumped up, but two men had left their seats and were moving towards us, blocking the aisle.

"This way," Emma said. She ran to the back of the bus, grabbed the metal hammer, and smashed it against the window. The glass shattered but stayed in place. I went towards her, but the conductor grabbed my pack. I held onto the seat backs in front of me, straining to move forward. Emma hit the window again, near the top, making a small hole. She hit it again and again, smashing holes along the top and down the side.

Behind me, the conductor shouted and pulled. My hands began to slip, so I let go and pushed myself backward. The conductor fell again, with me on top of him, but this time his head made a satisfying thump against the floor. Emma swung her pack at the window and the shattered glass fell away.

"Come on," she said.

I pulled myself up. Emma jumped out the window. I glanced behind me. The men were still there, deciding whether to get involved or not. No one else was moving. Farber's car was still in front of the bus, but Farber wasn't there.

Then Emma screamed.

I ran to the window. Farber was there, grappling with her. She'd dropped her pack. It was on the ground behind Farber. I jumped, but not on Farber, I went for the pack.

The fall wasn't far, but I slipped and hit the ground. Grabbing the pack, I jumped up, swung it, and smacked it against the side of Farber's head. He grunted but held on. His hat came off and I saw he had a bandage on his head. I went to hit him again but, still holding Emma by an arm, he reached into his coat with his free hand and came out with a gun. I swung the pack at it, but he pulled it aside and I missed. I continued the swing, spinning around to gain momentum and smashed the pack into the side of his leg.

This time, Farber yelped and fell, dragging Emma with him. The driver came out of the bus, a bulky man with a bulldog face and bristly hair.

"Hey, what are you playing at," he shouted.

Emma punched and kicked and scratched and I stamped on Farber's arm. He dropped his gun and Emma broke free.

Then something thudded on the ground behind me. I turned and saw the conductor.

"Run," Emma said.

We ran down the road.

"This way."

We cut into a field, heading towards a line of trees, the conductor close behind us.

"Get back here," he yelled.

"What do you think you're doing," the driver bellowed.

"Catching them," the conductor said. "They're getting away."

"That's his problem," the driver said. "I've got a schedule to keep. Get back on the bloody bus."

I glanced over my shoulder. The conductor had given up the chase and was heading towards the bus, but Farber was limping after us with the gun in his hand.

"Faster," I said.

We got to the trees well ahead of him, but the way was blocked by a tangle of bushes and briers. We bulled our way through them, using our packs to push them aside. They cut and scratched and ripped our clothes, but we made it through. Just ahead was a ravine with a wide stream at the bottom. We ran through the low weeds and slid down the gully.

I pulled Emma along, making sure we cut an obvious path. At the bottom, we splashed into the stream. When we'd gone about a hundred feet, I stopped.

"Up the other side," I said. "Now."

"What are you doing?" she asked. "If we follow the stream, we won't leave a trail."

"Exactly," I said. "Go up there. Hide behind a bush. Try not to leave a trail."

I ran on, making sure to tread on the bushes near the bank and step in the mud. When I was satisfied, I threw my flat cap in the water and ran a little farther. Then I went back towards Emma, running through the stream. Farber was at the edge of the wood. I stopped, climbed up the far side and hid behind a tree.

Farber picked his way through the brambles, using the path we had made, then followed our trail down the slope and along the stream until he found my cap. He was near enough to where I was hiding that I held my breath to keep from making any noise. He looked at my cap and the trail I'd left, while I pressed up against the tree, hoping he couldn't hear my heart pounding.

Farber looked around, up the far side of the gully, down the stream, up the stream. He stood and listened, then he kicked my hat, swore, and pointed the gun downstream, firing again and again until the revolver's hammer clicked on empty cylinders. The sound echoed through the gully and the smell of cordite filled the air.

He was unarmed now, and we could easily outrun him, but I remained hidden, waiting to see what he would do. He swore some more, kicked at the ground, and turned back, limping along the stream's edge. I was pleased to see that he struggled to climb up the side of the ravine. Then he disappeared through the brambles. I stayed where I was, listening. After a few moments, I heard movement, and saw Emma coming towards me.

"Oh my god," she said, hugging me. "I thought he'd shot you."

"No," I said, "he was just letting off some steam. I think we've lost him."

Emma's legs were cut and bleeding from the brambles. I had her sit on a rock at the stream's edge and washed her cuts with my hand.

"Here, use this," she said, pulling a handkerchief from her pocket. I dipped it in the cold water and wiped her legs, gently cleaning the blood and putting more cold water on her cuts until the bleeding stopped. I found it strangely soothing and pleasant. When I finished, I didn't want to stop, because it meant I would have to stop touching her.

"I think that's enough," she said.

I let go of her leg, my face hot. Then I cleaned my

own cuts, wrung out her handkerchief and gave it back to her. We climbed out of the ravine, up the side that Farber wasn't on, and walked through the trees and brush until we came to open land.

"Now where to?" I asked.

Emma shrugged. "Farber is to the west, and we don't want to go south or east, so north, I guess."

I looked up. It was only a little after noon, so the sun was high, but it still allowed me to judge direction. I pointed to where I thought north might be.

"This way, then?"

Emma nodded. "From train to bus to shank's pony," she said. "This is turning out to be some trip."

I fell into step beside her. Above, the drone of an airplane drew my attention. I looked up as a single Spitfire flew across the sky, heading east.

"Beautiful, isn't it," Emma said, also looking up.

It made me think of Mitch, and I wondered if he was still mad at me for leaving him behind, and how he was doing. I hoped he was having better luck than we were.

Chapter 25

Mitch

I couldn't believe it, but there it was, the unmistakable profile of a Dornier 17 bomber with two escorts. It was coming in from the Channel, flying high. A dozen questions flew through my mind. What was it doing here? Were there others? Had it become separated? Was anyone scrambling to intercept it? And, most importantly, what was I supposed to do about it?

It wasn't part of my mission. Should I avoid it and get back to base and report it? I had to decide fast, it was getting closer. I could now see the distinctive cross markings on the fuselage. Then it was decided for me. The Messerschmitts saw me and came streaking my way.

All questions, doubt, indecision, and fear left me. It was just me and my Spitfire, and I was going to have to fly for my life.

The lead Messerschmitt was close now. I headed straight towards it and fired off a quick burst. I was still too far away to hope for a hit, but it gave him something to think about as I pull the plane into a vertical climb. The Messerschmitt flew under me. I levelled out and saw the other Messerschmitt climbing to intercept me. I dived under it and headed for the bomber. Then I heard a burst of cannon-fire.

The first Messerschmitt was coming at me from behind. I turned left, then right. He stayed with me and fired again.

My heart pounded and, although it was cold in the cockpit, sweat ran down my spine. I had to shake him off or I'd be dead. I turned and turned again. He got closer. I pulled back on the stick, climbing, and the Messerschmitt followed. I flew straight up, and curved until the was ground above me and the sky below. Then I was heading down, increasing in speed, I kept on the same course, flying a tight loop until the Messerschmitt was in front of me.

I was so surprised I forgot to shoot. The pilot saw what had happened and took evasive action, turning and diving. I stayed behind him, gaining. I fired. The tat-tat of the guns joined the roar of the engine. The spirals of the tracer bullets streaked by the Messerschmitt's starboard side. I made a correction and fired again. The bullet trails moved closer, then cut across his tail section. A hit, but little damage. The Messerschmitt continued to turn one way, then the other trying to out-fly me. I stuck with him, centred him in my sight, and fired again. This time, the tracers streaked dead on and the bullets bored holes in the engine cowling. The Messerschmitt rolled on its side and plummeted towards the ground, trailing smoke and flames behind it.

Then I heard a thud and the plane shuddered as bullets slammed into the tail section. The other Messerschmitt was on me. I pulled up. Ahead of me, the bomber disappeared into a bank of clouds. I flew towards it and found myself enveloped in mist. I couldn't see the bomber, but the Messerschmitt couldn't see me, either. I pulled up, above the cloud, and looked around, but I couldn't see the Messerschmitt, or the bomber anywhere. I skimmed the top of the cloud, ready to dive down. Ahead, in a break in the cloud, the bomber became momentarily visible. I went back into the cloud and headed towards it.

My hands shook. I took a few deep breaths to calm myself. The cloud thinned and I, once again, caught sight of the bomber. And it caught sight of me. The tail guns fired. I pulled up, then pointed my nose at the bomber, firing as my plane dived towards it. The bullets went wide. I corrected my course and fired again, holding the trigger down, like James had told me not to do. A steady stream of tracers streaked towards the bomber, passing by its port side. I turned slightly, and watched the smoke trails get closer. Then holes appeared in the port wing, and bits of metal flew into the air as bullets pounded across the fuselage, along the starboard wing, and into the engine.

I let off and watched, mesmerized, as the engine smoked and burst into flames. The bomber began to descend, then it tipped on its side and headed towards the ground. I saw one, then two, then four parachutes open. I knew there would be more people on the plane who didn't get out, but I was glad that at least some did.

The tension drained from my body and sudden fatigue took over. Then I realized I had been flying straight and level for too long. I didn't think, or look around, I pulled the stick. But it was too late.

Bullets slammed into the side of the plane, hitting the engine and the wing. A final shot smashed through the cockpit in a sudden explosion of glass and metal. I jerked back into the seat, and everything went suddenly black as oil poured from the wrecked engine. Frantically, I wiped my goggles with oil-soaked gloves. It went black again. I wiped again. The plane was covered in oil. It pooled on the floor of the cockpit. I was so soaked with it I couldn't tell if I'd been hit or not.

My ears rang from the explosion but there was no other sound except for the rushing of wind through the shattered canopy. The engine had stopped. I was gliding and slowing down. Soon the plane would stall and spin to the ground with me trapped inside. I had to get out.

I tried to remember the bailout procedure. I was supposed to take off my helmet, but I was afraid oil might get in my eyes, so I yanked the wire and oxygen tube out, instead. I hit the harness release. What next? The canopy. I needed to open it. I reached up but it was jammed. The shot had twisted the metal. I punched out the last of the broken shards of acrylic until I thought I could squeeze through with my parachute on. Now I was supposed to roll the plane over so I would fall out, but there were no controls left to steer with.

I pulled myself up and tried to climb through the broken canopy. I pushed and kicked and strained, and my parachute got stuck. Then I saw the Messerschmitt circling around and lining up for another run. In a panic, I twisted and pulled and got unstuck, and inched further out of the cockpit. The Messerschmitt streaked towards me and began firing. I flopped out of the cockpit, onto the wing. The plane tipped under my weight as bullets ripped through the other wing, and I slid off the slick metal into open air.

White panic seized me. I fought to clear my mind. The force ripped the helmet from my head. I yanked my goggles off and suddenly I could see clearly. It didn't improve anything, though. I thought hard. There was a handle somewhere. I ran my gloved hand down my oily front. There it was. I gripped it and pulled.

The chute snaked out and unfurled, snapping in the wind. I felt a jerk as the silk caught the air and opened. Then I was floating instead of plummeting, but the ground still came towards me at an alarming speed, and I couldn't do anything about it. Trees zoomed by, a field, a shallow ravine. I hit the ground. The parachute dragged me into the gully, through the mud. I grabbed one of the ropes and pulled, hoping to collapse it. Then everything went still.

I tried to stand but my legs felt like jelly, and I fell to my hands and knees, drawing huge, gulping breaths, trying to calm myself. After a minute or two, I rose to my knees for a look around. I was in open land with brush and small trees and a muddy trench running through it that was probably a stream when it rained. I wasn't sure what to do. Go for help. Wait. Was I expected to bring the parachute back? It seemed the best thing to do, and it gave me a purpose.

Still on my knees, I began reeling the deflated canopy towards me. Then I heard a click behind me, and a voice said, "Don't move, or you're a dead man."

Chapter 26

Charlie

We walked through grassland for half an hour before we came to a road. It wasn't going in any direction we wanted so we left it behind and walked on until we came upon one that was heading north. The going was easier there, but it soon turned east so we went back to walking cross country, making sure we were heading more or less north.

"Shouldn't we be going west?" I asked. "That's where the Tor is."

"We don't want to go through Salisbury," Emma said. "We need to go around it. I'm not sure where we are, but if we keep going north, we'll eventually run into the A303. Then I'll know where we are and which way we should go."

"How far is the A303?"

"That I don't know."

"So, we just keep walking, then?"

"Unless you have a better idea."

The land wasn't hard to walk on, it was just hard to keep going north. There was a fair amount of open land, but there were also fields, which we had to skirt around. Sometimes there were paths, but other times there wasn't.

"I liked it better last time I was here," I said. "It was just grassland, as far as you could see."

Emma was walking beside me, her hands holding the straps of her pack. She turned her head to look at me. "When was that?"

"Depends."

"On what?"

"How you count time." I paused and let out a sigh. "For me, it was last year, but I suspect I was here sometime in the Middle Ages."

"Never!" She went quiet for a while. "What was it like?"

"The travelling was easier," I said. "I was on a horse."

She let the silence trail out. "But?"

I kept my eyes forward, focused on the ground. "There was a battle. It was horrific. Not something I like remembering."

"Sorry."

"Not your fault. You couldn't know."

"When were you here with Annie?"

"Two years ago," I said. "That's where Mitch learned to fly."

"Yes, she said you were very brave. Both of you."

"I thought we were incompetent."

She laughed. "Not in everything. She thinks you're heroes."

I shrugged. "I don't feel like a hero. Every time we go back, I'm scared to death."

"But you still go," she said. "That's the definition of a hero. True bravery is doing something you have to do even though you're scared."

"I guess so," I said, wishing she'd change the subject.

She didn't say anything for a while, and I hoped that was the end of it. Then she said. "I'm not a hero,

I'm just tagging along on your adventure. But I'm glad I am."

She stopped then.

I stopped a few steps ahead and turned to look at her.

"I'm glad you let me come," she said, as if she'd given me a choice. "This is the most alive I've ever felt." She stepped close. "And I think you're the most amazing person I have ever met."

Then she kissed me, smiled, and started walking again.

Stunned, I had to trot to catch up with her. She said nothing, but she took my hand, and we continued walking.

It took a while before we found another road, but it ran east and west so we crossed it and went back to open land. A short time later, we came to a railroad track. It was heading northeast and southwest, but it was easier to walk along it than go cross country again, so we followed the northeast route until we came to a crossing with a road heading north.

We made good time walking on the road. There were no cars but once, in the distance, I saw what looked like a military vehicle coming our way. We hid in the weeds and watched it go past. It was a jeep-like vehicle, with two MPs in the front seats.

"Do you think they're looking for us?" Emma asked.

"I expect so," I said. "Farrow is sure to have reported us by now. It's no secret we were in Portsmouth, and they must know we headed north."

We waited until the road was clear, then started walking again, but our progress was hampered because we had to keep looking over our shoulders to make sure no one was coming up behind us.

By now the sun was getting low. I was tired and hungry and wishing we were closer to the Tor. We left the road again and crossed more grassland and fields. In the distance, we saw a few houses, then a farm with several outbuildings and a large stone barn.

"That's perfect," Emma said.

We headed towards it, sinking low as we got closer. Crawling through the grass, we made it to the side of the barn. Then another jeep pulled into the farmyard. Two MPs got out. The door to the farmhouse opened and a woman stepped into view.

"Good afternoon," one of them said. "We're looking for two people. An RAF pilot and a girl. Have you seen anyone suspicious?"

The woman shook her head. "No. I haven't seen a soul all day."

"You don't mind if we have a look?"

"Of course not."

We backed deeper into the weeds and watched as the MPs went from building to building. Then they came to the barn. They were in there for a while, and we were close enough that we could hear them tramping around, going upstairs and down, and slamming doors.

"They must be doing a thorough search," Emma whispered.

I nodded and kept watching. After a while they returned to their vehicle and the woman came back outside. "Did you find anything?"

"No, but keep a sharp eye out. They were known to be headed this way."

The woman looked worried. "Are they dangerous?"

151

"I shouldn't think so. But if you see anyone, report it."

"I will."

Then they drove away, and we watched them head down the road to another farmhouse.

The woman went back inside, but we didn't dare move.

"She might be keeping a look out," I said. "Should we move on?"

"No," Emma said. "That barn is the perfect hiding place. It's already been searched."

We stayed in the grass, waiting for dark. Then another vehicle approached. A black car. It pulled into the farmyard, and Farber got out.

Chapter 27

Mitch

I raised my hands above my head. I didn't dare try to stand, so I squished through the mud on my knees, turning around to face whoever was behind me. A few yards away, standing at the top of the gully, was a man wearing overalls and a khaki jacket. His face was wrinkled, and grey hair stuck out from beneath a garrison cap. He was holding an old rifle, and pointing it straight at me.

"Keep your hands where I can see them." The rifle wavered in his hands, and I worried that his finger might slip on the trigger.

"I'm an RAF pilot," I said.

"So you say."

"I can prove it," I said, lowering my hands slowly. "Just let me get out of this sidcot suit,"

He steadied the rifle. "Don't you move, unless you want a bullet in your gut."

I put my hands back up.

"Really, I am," I said. "I'm speaking English, aren't I?"

"Krauts know how to speak English."

"But I have an American ... I mean, a Canadian accent."

"So, you're a Kraut who speaks English in a Canadian accent. Keep your hands up or you'll be a dead Kraut."

I sighed. "Then turn me in."

"That'll come."

He said nothing after that. I sat back on my heels. My arms began to ache, and I struggled to keep them up.

Soon, another soldier came running our way. A young man without a weapon.

"What have you got, Howard?" he asked, gasping for breath.

"Kraut. Saw four of them bail out of that Dornier 17."

"I'm an RAF pilot," I said.

"He says he's RAF," the young man said.

"That's his story," Howard said. "I didn't see any of our planes go down."

"I'm Pilot Officer Johnny Kent," I said, "with the one eight eight Squadron, Horsham. Contact them. They'll know who I am."

"He sure sounds like an RAF pilot," the younger man said.

"Well, I'm not giving him the benefit of the doubt. Go tell the Captain I've got me a Kraut. Tell him to get here sharpish."

The young man ran off. While Howard was watching him, I laced my hands behind my head. It was a lot more comfortable. Howard turned back but didn't say anything. I waited. My ankle began to throb, and I wondered if I had been hit or if I had hurt it landing. I couldn't check, though, as Howard kept the rifle pointed my way, and I didn't want to give him any excuse to shoot me.

After what seemed like an hour, I heard a vehicle approaching. I looked and saw a jeep, with two RAF men in it, bumping through the field as it raced towards us. Howard didn't move. He kept his eye looking down the rifle sight at me. The jeep stopped hard behind Howard, skidding over the grass. The men jumped out.

"Kent, is that you?" It was James.

"Yes," I shouted, relieved.

The other man was the pilot they called Yo-Yo. They jumped into the gully and pulled me to my feet.

"We thought you were a goner," James said.

"That's my prisoner," Howard yelled. "Leave him be, he might be dangerous."

They ignored him. I tried to take a step and would have fallen if they hadn't grabbed me.

"My ankle," I said.

"Shot?" James asked.

"Don't know," I said. "I haven't been able to look."

James looked at Howard, who still had his rifle trained on us.

"If you don't put that rifle down," he said, drawing his revolver, "I'll become dangerous."

Howard stepped back, a disgusted look on his face, but he lowered the rifle, and I breathed a sigh of relief.

They helped me to the jeep and put me in the back.

"What happened?" James asked.

"Rookie mistake," I said. "I forgot to count to ten."

Chapter 28

Charlie

We sank low in the weeds.

"What's with that guy?" I asked. "How does he keep finding us?"

"We need to go," Emma said.

I grabbed her arm.

"No, wait. He can't know we're here. Let's see what he wants."

Farber didn't look our way. Instead, he went towards the house, limping slightly. He had his hat on with the bandage just visible below its brim. He knocked on the door. The woman answered.

"I'm looking for two fugitives," he said.

The woman looked surprised, and a little wary. "The MPs were just here," she told him. "They headed towards the Anderson's. You might catch them there."

Farber shook his head. "I'm not with the MPs. I'm from the Government. These fugitives are wanted urgently. They are dangerous and should not be approached."

"My goodness," the woman said. "What should I do?"

Farber glanced around the farmyard. We held our breath. "Nothing. But if you see two young people together, a boy and a girl, call this number."

He handed a card to the woman. She took it and put it in her apron pocket.

"They both have red hair," he said, "and the boy speaks with a Canadian accent. If you report them, and your information leads to their arrest, you will receive a handsome reward, as well as your country's gratitude."

Without another word, he left. The woman watched him get into his car and drive away in the same direction as the MPs. She pulled the card from her pocket and stared at it as she slowly closed the door.

"He's following the MPs," I said. "He wants to make sure he gets to us before they do."

"It's going to be hard going" Emma said. "If anybody sees us, they'll be only too glad to have a chance at that reward."

We laid side by side in the tall grass, watching the house. No one stirred.

"Should we go?" I asked.

Emma looked at me like I had suggested we should try flapping our arms to see if we could fly to the Tor. "Go where? If we expose ourselves, someone is sure to spot us. Someone has probably already told the MPs, or Farber, they saw us walking this way."

"What then?"

"That barn is still our best hiding place. They won't search it again, not for a while."

I had to agree, but we also had to get into it without being seen. We couldn't wait for dark, as the farmer would be coming home at some point, and we didn't know where he would go. For all he knew, he'd be coming across the field straight at us.

We crawled away from the house and circled behind the barn. There wasn't a back door, but there was a window. We pulled it open and looked inside. It was dark and dusty. There were benches covered in tools, and hanging from the walls were rakes and shovels and leather things that Emma told me belonged to horses. It looked empty so we squeezed inside.

The air smelled of old hay and fresh manure. In the corner I saw a section surrounded by a partition about five feet tall. Inside, the floor was covered in hay.

"That looks like a good hiding place," I said.

Emma cupped her face in her hands and shook her head. "That's where the horse sleeps," she said.

I looked around. "What horse?"

"Exactly. We need to get out of here before the farmer comes back. He'll have a horse, and he'll put it there."

Then came the sound of hooves clopping on the road. We froze. The clopping slowed and came nearer, accompanied by the creaking of a wagon. It had taken a while to get in through the window; we didn't have enough time to get out.

"Quick, up the stairs," Emma said.

We ran to the stairs and climbed them as quietly as we could. Upstairs was an open room. The floor was strewn with hay and there was a small pile against the far wall. Above was a pitched roof, with rafters and crossbeams, but there was no way to get up there, and no place to hide if we did. Then we saw the huge opening in the wall, giving us a view of the house, and the house a view of us. We dropped to the floor and crawled to the far corner where we were out of sight.

Then we took off our packs and sat, leaning against the rough wall, breathing as quietly as we could.

The cart stopped just outside the barn, below the big opening. I heard clicking and clacking and the horse neighing, and then I heard the horse being led to the far corner of the lower level, into the stable I had wanted to hide in. Emma said nothing, but she looked at me and smirked.

After signalling to Emma by holding a finger to my lips, I laid on the floor and peered through a gap in the boards. There appeared to be two people, a man and a boy. The boy combed down the horse while the man hung up the harness and bridle. When the horse was settled and the gear put away, they went back to the wagon.

"I'll pitch it up," the man said, "you pile it."

"Yessir," the boy said.

Fast footsteps across the floor, and up the stairs. We barely had time to grab our packs and dive under the hay. We laid together, hoping we were covered. The hay was full of dust and pollen, and it was all I could do not to sneeze. Emma pulled the handkerchief out of her pocket and breathed through it. She moved close to me. We put our faces together and stretched the cloth so it covered both our noses and mouths. I breathed slowly, trying to calm myself.

A thud sounded nearby. Then a scrape and a thump, and more dust stirred around us. They were emptying the wagon, the man pitching hay into the barn through the big opening, and the boy forking it into a big pile on top of us. We laid as still as we could, breathing slowly, trying not to cough.

I heard the woman shout from the house about teatime and the man answer that they were nearly

159

done. More thuds, thumps, and dust. Finally, it stopped. The boy walked to another corner. I heard him moving hay around and started to panic. Emma whispered in my ear, "He's feeding the horse."

I nodded and we waited. More footsteps and thumping, and what little light there was disappeared. Then the boy went downstairs. We heard the wagon roll inside. The doors swung closed with a bang. A latch clicked into place. We stayed frozen, listening.

"Do you think it's safe yet," I asked.

Emma nodded.

We crawled out from under the hay. What had been a small pile was now a larger pile, and the big opening was covered with a wooden shutter. I peered through the cracks between the boards. Emma put her face next to mine. "What do you see?"

"It's starting to get dark," I said. "There are lights on in the house. No one is outside."

"I guess that means we're safe."

I leaned back. "For now."

Emma sat on the hay. "All we have to do is get out of here before the farmer catches us, and somehow get all the way to Glastonbury without being seen."

I sat next to her, feeling suddenly tired. "Yes," I said, "and I have no idea how we're going to do that."

Chapter 29

Mitch

"You're grounded, pending an investigation, after which you will be court marshalled."

"What?"

"Did I give you permission to speak?"

I swallowed hard. "No, sir."

Farrow smiled, but it didn't make him look any less menacing.

I'd hoped I could go to the barracks and take a nap once they brought me back, but after showering and changing into a fresh uniform, I'd been taken to the infirmary.

The doctor had checked me over and said I'd sprained my ankle. He told me that, all things considered, I'd gotten off lightly. I agreed. Then I was ordered to report to Commander Farrow, so I limped to the Headquarters hut, expecting to be commended. Instead, he wanted to arrest me.

"If I may ask, sir, what for?"

Farrow took a pen and began rolling it between his hands. "You were on a training flight. Am I wrong?"

"No, sir."

"You were to fly a specified route and return to base. With a plane. Is that correct?"

"Yes, sir."

"Do you have a plane with you?"

"Well, no sir. I was shot down."

He laid the pen on the desk and leaned forward. "Poppycock."

I felt my face grow hot.

"You got lost and you ran out of fuel and crashed."

"No, sir. I was involved in combat."

Farrow shook his head. "You take me for a fool, son?"

I said nothing.

"Well, do you?" he asked.

"No sir."

"A training flight does not involve combat. You did not follow orders. You lost a valuable aircraft and now you want me to believe it was because you were in combat."

"That's the truth, sir."

Farrow's eyes narrowed. "I don't like you, Mr. Kent. There's something not right with you. Our Mr. Farber took a keen interest in you and your friend. Then you let your friend desert. And now Mr. Farber is out looking for him. There must be something quite special about him, and you, to make Mr. Farber so interested, don't you agree?"

I took a breath, trying to calm myself. I wished I had James or Fulbright with me for support, but they had left in a jeep as soon as I had been brought back to the base.

"That's nothing to do with me, sir," I said. "Richard Hamlin was simply posted here the same time I was."

Farrow sat back and started tapping the pen on his desk. "It's too much of a coincidence, your friend deserting, and you destroying a Spitfire. If I had my

162

way, I'd have you shot. As it is, you'll get away with being court marshalled and detained at His Majesty's pleasure."

I wanted to tell him that wasn't fair, but it would sound like I was whining.

Farrow pulled a sheet of paper from a drawer and began writing on it. "Failure to follow orders. You were to fly, as ordered, and return, as ordered. You did neither. And now you're lying to try to save yourself."

Anger surged through me. I clenched my fists.

"Sergeant," Farrow shouted.

An MP came forward and stood to attention next to me.

"Take this prisoner to the cells."

"Yes, sir."

Then I heard a knock on the door. Farrow ignored it, but the door opened, and someone entered. Farrow looked up and scowled. "I am busy. You can see me once I finish here."

"Apologies, sir. But you need to hear this." It was Fulbright's voice. I relaxed my hands and the tension eased from my shoulders.

"I need to hear nothing, Squadron Leader. I am dealing with a prisoner."

But Fulbright ignored him. He marched across the room and stood next to me. "Pilot Officer Kent is not lying, sir."

Farrow laid the pen on the paper and sat back, frowning.

"I've just returned from the crash site," Fulbright said. "A Messerschmitt and a Dornier 17 bomber both crashed in fields south of here. The survivors from the bomber have confirmed that Kent shot both planes down. We found the wreckage of his Spitfire in a wooded area nearby. It was shot full of holes."

Farrow's lips compressed into a thin, white line. "I don't expect a pilot on a training exercise to engage in combat."

"With respect, sir, if Pilot Officer Kent ignored a bomber and its escorts in order to complete a training run, and that bomber destroyed property and killed civilians, I would court martial him myself. He did what he was trained to do. I would expect no less from any of my men."

Farrow shook his head and sighed. "All right. Dismissed."

"Sir," the MP said. "Am I still to escort the prisoner—"

"No," Farrow shouted. "Now get out, all of you."

We saluted and walked out. My foot was throbbing, but I did my best not to limp.

Outside, the MP smiled and saluted me. "Well done, son," he said.

I returned his salute. "Thanks."

"That was some bit of flying you did," Fulbright said, when the MP left us. "We interviewed some people on the ground who had seen it. You did splendidly. Until you were shot down."

"Yes, sir," I said. "I'll try harder next time. And sorry about the plane."

Fulbright smiled. "We have more airplanes than men. I'd rather have you back in one piece than go down with the Spitfire. Now, I believe you deserve a drink."

I hesitated, thinking I'd rather have a nap.

"That's an order, son," Fulbright said, already leading the way.

We walked to the Officers' Club. As soon as we opened the door, all conversation stopped. The only sound in the smoky room was the radio playing in the background. All the other pilots were there, sitting around tables, drinks in their hands. When they saw us, they stood and applauded.

"Take a seat," Fulbright said. "I'll get you a pint."

As I walked forward, the men gathered around me, pumping my hand, and slapping me on the back as they escorted me to a table. James was there. He pulled a seat out for me, and I sat next to him.

"Great going," Ziggy said, looming over me. "You're quite the gunner."

Yo-Yo grabbed my arm. "You doubled our kill score in one afternoon. Nice shooting, Gunner."

Then Fulbright was there handing me a pint glass. I took a few, tentative sips.

"To Gunner!" the men shouted, and they all drank.

I took a few more sips and, as before, the beer began to taste good.

Fulbright sat on the other side of me. The men encouraged me to tell them about my escapade, so I started telling my story. It seemed like a fantasy; here I was, an RAF pilot, at the start of the Battle of Britain, swapping stories and sharing drinks with the most famous warriors in history. My head felt light, and it wasn't just from the beer. I was part of the group. At last, I felt like I belonged.

The vision the Talisman had shown me attempted to push to the forefront of my mind, but I wouldn't let it. That was for another time. I found it easy to ignore; it wasn't much different from what the other men—boys, really—grappled with themselves. It

165

didn't make me special, it made me just like them—an airman enjoying another celebration and not thinking about the morning. The future would take care of itself. Tonight, there was just this, and I didn't want to be anywhere else, not ever.

Chapter 30

Charlie

It was dark outside, and darker in the barn. We didn't turn on the flashlight for fear we'd be seen, and there wasn't anything we really needed light for, anyway. Looking through the gaps in the boards, I saw the lights in the house turn off, one by one.

"It appears they're bedding down for the night," I said.

We decided to do the same. We'd need to rise early to get out before the farm came to life. In the dark, we made a nest in the hay, laid down on the blanket and covered up with the cloak.

"Good night," I said.

Emma said nothing. She kissed me, instead.

I laid on my back, looking up at the darkness, wondering what I should do.

"Kissing cousins," Emma said.

"What?"

"Kissing cousins. That's what Annie said she and Mitch were. So, I guess that's what we are."

"I guess so," I said.

"Are we really cousins?"

I thought about it for a while. "I suppose. According to the genealogy Granddad gave us, we're related somehow."

I heard a rustle next to me as she turned on her

side. "If you have a genealogy, do you know when I … I mean, how long I live?"

"No," I said. "It isn't set up like that. It's just a straight line, from me and Mitch to Dad to Granddad and on up to John—who was my great, great, great, great grandfather—and then on to Baron someone or other. That's where it ends. But we know that the Baron was descended from Aelric, who we met in 1066. He had to leave Sussex because of the Normans, which is why you all live in Lancashire. Aelric was a descendant of Pendragon. We met him on our first adventure, and on our last. We didn't know we were related to him when we first met him, and when we saw him the second time, we found out he was Arthur's grandson."

Emma remained quiet for a while. I was glad for the darkness; I didn't want to see her looking at me with utter disbelief.

"I'm related to Arthur?" she asked after a few minutes of silence. "King Arthur? *The* King Arthur?"

"Yeah. Distantly. Like me."

"He's real?"

"I met him. Twice." I didn't tell her that I had watched him die, or what the circumstances of our meetings involved.

"But he's a legend. You can't be related to a legend."

"Real people become legends," I said, "and I'd better be related to him. Only a descendant of Arthur can put the Talisman back in its place. I'm pretty sure that's why I'm here."

"This is … I'm glad you didn't mention this when we first met."

"Don't worry," I said. "I hardly believe it myself.

And I'd never believe it if I hadn't seen it with my own eyes, so you're doing better than me."

She thumped me on the shoulder. "I didn't say I believed it," she said, laughing.

"Are you saying I'm a liar?"

"No," she said, moving her face close enough to mine where I could feel her breath. "You're not a liar. You're my cousin."

"Distant cousin," I said.

"Distant enough?"

I wanted to say yes, but her lips covered my mouth and all I could do was mumble.

After a few moments, she pulled away, "So, we are kissing cousins, then?"

I put my arms around her and kissed her back. "Yes, and I'm glad."

"Me too."

We held each other in the dark, safe for the moment. I hugged her tight and kissed her, trying to keep any thoughts of what might be waiting for us out of my head. The Talisman hadn't shown me much, it was mostly a feeling, a feeling that was the opposite of what I was feeling now. I pushed it from my mind and thought only about her, the warmth of her body, the caress of her hands, the feel of her lips, and the giddy knowledge that I wanted this to go on forever.

Chapter 31

Mitch

The next morning, early, we were scrambled. We rushed through breakfast, then got suited and checked our planes. My foot throbbed but I did my best to not let it show. My head throbbed worse, but everyone seemed to be suffering from that, so it wasn't as bad.

After all the checks were done, orders came for Flight One to join up with six oh one Squadron for a possible intercept. Those of us remaining watched them take off, roaring across the field in the cool dawn. Then we waited some more, and Yellow section was ordered up to search for an enemy reconnaissance plane reported to be in the area. That left only James and me to watch them take off, and soon after we were told to stand down for the rest of the day.

"Kent isn't cleared to fly," Fulbright told James, "and there's no use sending you up on your own."

So, we took off the Sidcot suits, put everything away, and went back to the barracks. We were the only ones there. I tried to take a nap, but James was restless, pacing and muttering. I knew he wanted to go up and I knew it was my fault he couldn't so, since I wasn't going to get any sleep, I decided to go outside and find something constructive to do.

I wandered back to the hangers to admire my new Spitfire, and saw the crew working on her, turning the engine and polishing the propeller.

Chief Mechanic Roddis nodded to me. "Not flying today, sir?"

"No," I said. "Doctor grounded me. Hurt my foot yesterday."

Roddis chuckled and kept fiddling with the engine. "Lucky that was all you hurt, sir."

I stood behind him, feeling slightly awkward. I didn't like being called 'sir,' not by men older, more experienced, and smarter than me. After a few minutes, I cleared my throat.

"Something on your mind, sir?" he asked.

"Is there any way I can make myself, um, useful?"

Roddis turned and gave me a strange look, a mixture of curiosity and pity, with a dash of annoyance thrown in.

"Sir," he said, "I'm the NCO, I do the useful things. You're an officer." Then he smiled and winked and turned back to his work.

I hobbled away, back towards the barracks. Along the edge of the runway, away from the hangers and the airplanes, I saw a freshly dug ditch. It didn't look like a drainage ditch, and I couldn't think of any other use for it, so I assumed it was one of those military things that the lower ranks did, digging holes and then refilling them, but there was no pile of fresh earth to put back in the hole. I ignored it and walked across the runway, past the windsock, and saw another ditch. This one was fresher, and there was a pile of dirt next to it with two shovels sticking out of it. The hole was long, narrow, and neatly squared off, just like the ones I'd had to dig when I'd been in other armies. It

171

brought a wave of nostalgia and, before I knew what I was doing, I grabbed a shovel and began refilling the hole.

I had barely begun when I heard someone shouting. I turned and saw two privates, or airmen, or whatever they called the lowest ranks in the RAF, running towards me, each pushing a wheelbarrow.

"What the bloody hell are you playing at?"

The two men came closer, sputtering and swearing, then they suddenly stopped, stood to attention, and saluted. "Sorry, sir," one of them said, "but, with respect, what do you think you're doing?"

I felt heat rise up my neck into my cheeks and knew I was turning red. "I thought I was …" I looked at the hole and the dirt and the wheelbarrow. "I guess I misunderstood. You see …"

But what could I say? That I'd watched this sort of duty in 1916? That I'd been a raw recruit in Elizabeth's army in 1588, and had marched with king Alfred's men in 1066?

"I was just trying to help," I said. "Bring the wheelbarrows closer, I'll help fill them."

The men shook their heads, looking worried. "Sir, we can't, you can't do that."

"Well, I know it's not my job, but I do know how to shovel, and—"

"Kent, what the hell do you think you're doing?"

I looked and saw James running from the barracks, racing down the road, waving his arms. The two men looked relieved.

James arrived, took the shovel from me and handed it to one of the men. "You can't do this, Kent."

I looked at the ground, then at the two men who

were still staring at me in disbelief. "Sorry," I said, "I guess I misunderstood. I thought you were doing fatigue duty."

"Fatigue?" one of them said.

James took me by an arm. "You'll have to forgive him," he said to the men. "He's from Canada. They do things differently there."

The men nodded but didn't seem convinced.

"Come on, Kent," James said, "let's get back to the—"

Then the barracks exploded.

Chapter 32

Charlie

It was dark in the barn when I woke up, but grey light was visible between the gaps in the boards covering the big window. I untangled myself from Emma, got dressed, and put my eye up to one of the cracks. I'd hoped we could get away before the family woke up, but a farmer's day starts early and there were already lights on in the house. The farmer and the boy came out the door and headed across the farmyard.

"Emma, wake up," I said, running back to her.

"Wha—"

"Farmer's coming."

She jumped up, squirming into her skirt and pulling on her blouse. Together, we stuffed the cloak into my backpack, fluffed up the hay and crawled underneath it. Within seconds, I heard banging down below as the doors were unlatched and pushed open. The horse stirred, hooves clopped, wood creaked. We waited.

There were footsteps on the stairs, and we held our breath. Suddenly, the barn became much lighter. Then the footsteps retreated, back down the stairs, and the horse, cart and, hopefully, the farmer and the boy, drove away.

I looked through the hay. We were alone. The big

opening was uncovered. and the wooden shutter was leaning against the wall next to it.

"They'll be getting more hay," Emma said. "We need to leave."

We put on our packs and tiptoed down the stairs. The doors were closed so the light was dim, but that kept us from being seen from the house. We went to the window, threw our packs through it, and climbed out after them.

We went back to the field, keeping low even though the light was still dim and there didn't appear to be anyone around. On the far side of the field was a creek and we followed that for a while, until we came to a road. It was a narrow country lane, crossing the creek over a stone bridge. We climbed up and decided to follow the road. It was easier going, but we had to keep a look-out for cars or horses, and several times had to dive into the weeds to avoid being seen. It wasn't long before the little road led to a bigger road. It was wide and paved and open, providing little cover. It was also busier, and we found we had to hide in the bushes as we struggled to figure out where we were.

"This is the A303," Emma said, once traffic had cleared long enough for her to have a good look.

Unfortunately, she wasn't exactly sure where on the A303 we were. I told her it didn't matter; we just needed to travel west, but she told me it drifted south, and we'd miss the Tor by miles if we stayed on it. We stood on the edge of the road, facing each other, watching for traffic, and I got a strange feeling.

"I think I know where I am," I said.

"How?"

Surrounding us were fields and gently undulating

land. There were lines of trees and hedges that were new but if I blanked them out and imagined them as unbroken grassland, it began to feel familiar. "I've been here before," I said, "several times."

"Are you sure?"

Without answering, I crossed to the far side of the road and walked into a field. Emma followed. "Where are you going?"

I led us through a row of low trees bordering a field and in the far distance, on a rise, stood an unmistakable landmark.

"That's Stonehenge," Emma said.

I nodded, "We passed this way, travelling to and from the Tor."

"How far are we away from the Tor, then?"

I shrugged. "Two days," I said, "but we had horses. On foot, it'll be more like three. Back then, we followed the ancient paths."

"Can you find them now?"

"I don't know, but we can look."

We walked across the open land, to the grey stones. It was now full daylight, with clouds covering the sky. In the sombre light, the monument seemed to brood. It was just as silent and empty as it had been centuries before, with one slight difference.

"It's in a lot worse shape than the first time I saw it."

Emma ran her hand over one of the massive, fallen lintels. "When was that."

I took her hand and led her through the centre of the circle. "Sometime in the late Roman period," I said, not stopping. "The Druids brought us here."

"What for? Some kind of ceremony?"

I laughed. "You could say that. We were supposed

to be sacrificed."

I kept us walking through the circle, in a direction that felt familiar. I had expected Emma to be shocked or curious, but she kept silent until we'd left the stones behind.

"I take it they didn't," she said, at last, "sacrifice you."

I looked around. Fields and grassy plains and not a person in sight. I wondered how long we could count on that. I tried to imagine it as it was back then, and found it wasn't too difficult.

"No," I said. "Kayla saved us. Otherwise, I wouldn't be here."

We kept walking, and I struggled to remember the last time I had been here, and the direction we had gone in. It wasn't long before we found a path. Then the path became a lane, and the lane a road.

"Seems like the ancient paths are now roads," I said. "We passed this way in 1066, when we fought in the Battle of Hastings with Aelric, and again last year, on our way to meet Arthur."

After a while, we saw a village, so we detoured around it, walking through fields and pastures for an hour before rejoining the road. It was easier walking on the road, except that we had to be alert for cars. When we heard one, we hid in the bushes until it passed. Fortunately, there weren't many.

"How do you manage?" Emma asked after a long silence.

"What do you mean?"

"Having done all that? How do you just go back to your home and go to school and have dinner with your family and live a normal life?"

"It's not hard, or at least, it wasn't. The

adventures, as we call them, always faded to a dream, so we really didn't remember them. It wasn't until the next summer, when Grandfather sent us the next gift, that the memories would resurface, but even then, we thought they were just some sort of hallucination. Until the feather."

"Annie's feather?"

"Yes. It was the only thing that has ever come back with us, and then we knew it was all real. Before that, we used to argue about going. One of us usually wanted to forget it. But once we knew it was real, we felt we had to go."

Emma laughed. "When you thought it was just a dream, you didn't want to go. But when you knew it was real, and dangerous, you went anyway."

"We had to; we knew it was important."

"And what happened with the feather? Once you knew it was all real?"

"Mitch became mad about flying. He really took to it in 1916. He's probably having the time of his life flying with your brother."

"And you?"

"I just dreaded the next summer. Then it came, and we went, and it was really awful. But when we got home, we were sure it was over, and we were so relieved. Then, this year, we got the Talisman, and we realized this was going to be our most important adventure yet."

Emma stopped and turned to face me. "Charlie, I want to give you something. Something you can keep with you. Something that you can take back with you."

She took her handkerchief from her pocket and placed it in my hand. I opened it up, looking at the pink stains from her blood. "What makes you think it will work?"

"Why did the feather go back?"

I folded the handkerchief and put it in my pocket. "I don't know. We couldn't—"

"I think it was because they were in love."

She took my hands in hers and looked at me, her eyes sparkling. "You are the bravest person I have ever met." She leaned in to kiss me, but then she stopped, and her eyes opened wide in alarm.

Chapter 33

Mitch

I ducked as hunks of wood and rock rained down on us, then the sound of airplanes filled the sky. The high whine of a siren cut through the din. Men ran, shouting. Then another explosion, this time in the runway. The blast knocked me sideways. Smoke and the smell of gunpowder swirled around me. I scrambled to my feet and saw I was alone. The only part of the barracks left standing was the stone section from the old house, the same wall that had survived the bombing in 1916. I figured they must have run there for cover and started to follow them.

More explosions and shouts. High above I heard a sound I recalled from old World War Two films, the scream of what they called a Jericho Trumpet, which meant that Stuka bombers were diving on us. I ran faster, then was tackled from behind. I looked and saw James gripping my legs.

"What the bloody hell are you doing?" he shouted.

A Stuka dived for us, its guns rat-tatting, the shells kicking up dirt in a line that streaked by us.

"Going for cover."

"Then get in the slit trench."

"The what?"

James dragged me to my feet. "The hole you were trying to fill in."

We ran back to the hole. The other two men were in it, lying on top of one another. James pushed me in as another bomb shook the ground. I fell on top of the two men, and James fell on top of me.

All I could hear were explosions, shouts, and screams. Smoke drifted over us, making me choke. It was hard to breathe with James lying on me, but I was glad I wasn't the guy at the bottom. The boom of anti-aircraft artillery sounded, the ground shook as more bombs hit, then slowly, the roar of airplanes faded.

"Is it safe?" I asked.

"I bloody well hope so," the man at the bottom said. "I can't breathe."

We climbed out of the hole. Smoke wafted across the runway, now pocked with several large craters. A few buildings were damaged, and one of the hangers was on fire. Men ran in every direction, shouting orders.

"The Spitfires," James shouted. "Come on."

We ran through the smoke towards the hanger. A crowd of men were already there. One had a hose trained on a burning airplane, others flailed at the flames with blankets, shovels, rakes, or their own jackets.

We joined a line of men handing buckets to the men up front. Even from where I stood the heat was intense. I didn't know how the front men were able to stand it, but they dumped bucket after bucket on the flames while the hose continued to spray water on the Spitfire. Slowly, the flames died out. Soon, we could all get closer. The plane was damaged beyond repair, its wings twisted, the landing gear buckled, but they kept dousing it with water, and I realized they were trying to keep it from exploding.

Steam hissed, smoke billowed, but the flames were out. I coughed and wiped the sting of smoke from my eyes.

"I think we got it," James said. "If that had exploded, it would have taken out another half dozen. We were lucky."

We stepped back from the blackened hanger and the ruined airplane and looked towards the runway. There were several large craters, and a few smaller ones, scatter from one end to the other.

"The squadron will need to land soon," James said. "We've got to fill those in. Come on."

He shouted for the other men to join us. We grabbed shovels and rakes and went to the largest crater. Other men joined us, and James divided the men up, sending half to another hole.

"Fill the ones on the left side first," he told them. "They'll be able to land on half the runway while we fix the other side."

Men arrived at a run, pushing wheelbarrows filled with gravel. We raked and shovelled and dumped gravel, but it still wasn't level. More gravel, more shovelling. Fulbright arrived shouting more orders, but he, too, grabbed a shovel and pitched in. Farrow, I noticed, was nowhere to be seen.

The sound of incoming aircraft made us all stop and look up, ready to run, but it was the squadron, coming in.

"Hurry," James said.

When the hole was as level as we could make it, we ran to another, and another.

The planes lined up to land and we retreated to the other side of the runway, panting and gasping, covered in dirt, soot, and sweat.

The first plane touched down and bounced over the field, wobbling as it rolled over the newly filled craters, but it made it down safely. Another followed, and another.

A sense of calm began to descend. I looked around at the damaged buildings and the burned-out hanger.

"I'd say we got off lightly." It was Fulbright, still holding a shovel. "Good job with the fire. That could have spelled disaster. As it is, we just need to finish fixing the runway." Then he looked at the ruined barracks. "And find a place for you to sleep tonight."

Chapter 34

Charlie

"What is it?"

Emma dropped my hands. "A truck."

"MPs?" I asked, panic rising in my chest.

"No, just a truck."

"Can we hide?"

Emma shook her head. "They'll have seen us by now. If we try to hide, it will seem suspicious."

"Then keep walking. If we ignore them, they might ignore us."

We walked single file to allow the truck room to pass on the narrow road. As it came up behind us, I held my breath. It drove by, and I let it out, feeling relief as the panic subsided. Then the truck stopped.

I'd have said it was a pickup truck if there had been sides and a tailgate, but the back end was simply a flatbed made of boards. A wooden box, tied down with twine to keep it from sliding off, was the only cargo. There were no fenders on the back wheels, and the cab was speckled with rust. Through the cracked back window, I saw the driver—the only occupant—lean across the front seat to roll the passenger window down.

"What's he doing?" I asked Emma, keeping my voice low.

"He's going to offer us a lift," she whispered back.

"Should we take it?"

I shrugged. "It's a risk, but at least we'll make better time."

"Then let me get in first. I'll do the talking."

When we reached the truck, Emma looked through the open window.

"Where you heading?" the man at the wheel asked. His shaggy hair was flecked with grey, and the sleeves of his flannel shirt were rolled up to his elbows, showing muscular forearms.

Emma pointed down the road. "That way."

The man chuckled. "There's a whole lot of nothing up that way, but you'll get there quicker if you're not walking."

Emma opened the door and slid onto the bench seat. I crammed in beside her, slammed the door and rolled the window up. The man jammed the truck into gear. Then it lurched forward and sped down the road.

"My name's Gerry Buckham," he said, looking Emma over when he should have been keeping his eyes on the road.

"Trish," Emma said. "Trish Norton, and this is my brother, Charlie."

It jarred that she used my real name, but then she was used to it, and no one was looking for Charlie Norton.

"So, Trish Norton, where you heading?"

Emma looked out the dusty windshield. "Shepton Mallet."

Buckham whistled through his teeth. "You'd be walking a day and a night to get there if I hadn't picked you up."

Emma smiled at him. "And we're ever so grateful.

185

We've been living with our aunt in Salisbury, working there, but with the war on, we're going back to see our mum. Then we're signing up. I'm going to be a Land Girl."

Gerry bobbed his head. "That so, girl? And what about you, son? What do you plan to be?"

"A soldier, sir," I said, keeping my words short.

Buckham nodded, seemingly satisfied. He drove for a while, saying nothing. I started to get uncomfortable with the pack pressing into my back. I felt like taking it off, like Emma had (she now carried hers in her lap, covering her legs) but I didn't want to do anything to draw attention.

"I'll tell you what," Buckham said after a while. "My place is outside Warminster. Were I to let you off there, you'd be walking well into dark. Why not come to my place? I could use some help, what with my boy away with the army. Then I could drive you the rest of the way in the morning."

It sounded too good to be true and I mistrusted the idea immediately. It was, however, a deal we couldn't pass up. It would look suspicious if we turned it down, and the thought of getting to the Tor quicker made it a chance worth taking. I looked sideways at Emma and nodded.

"That would be grand, Mr. Buckham," she said. "Thank you so much."

Buckham chuckled. "Call me Gerry."

◆

It turned out that Warminster was ten miles away, and Shepton Mallet (seven miles from Glastonbury) another fifteen miles after that, which made it a total of thirty-two miles, give or take, from where we were to the Tor. That made me feel more kindly to the offer of a ride, even if I had to do some work for it. My problem was, I had to somehow keep my mouth shut the whole time. I hoped he might send me into a field to hoe, then I could claim I was too tired for dinner and just go to sleep until the next day.

As it was, I didn't have to worry too much. Buckham liked to talk, and he didn't seem to need my input to encourage him.

"Charlie, you untie that box in back, and take it to that building there," Buckham said as soon as he pulled into his yard.

He lived on a small farm that he and his son ran until his son joined up, and Buckham was in favour of that, all right, but it did make his life hard, especially since his mule died earlier that summer. The farm was small, but it had been his dad's, and his dad's dad's before him, and he was bound to leave it to his son, so he wanted to make some improvements, but that wasn't easy with the war on and it sure was good of us to help him out.

All this came out as we trundled up the narrow lane to his small farmyard, where there was a stone and brick house with ivy clinging to it and shutters hanging askew. Scattered around were several outbuildings, some brick, some wooden. The one Buckham had pointed out—the one he wanted me to take the box to— was small, made of brick, and had a thick, wooden door.

"And treat it gentle, mind," he said as I got out of the cab, "you don't want it going off."

I climbed onto the back and began undoing the twine while Buckham led Emma into the house. I was

187

a little nervous about that, but I assumed she could take care of herself, or at least scream for help. When I got the twine loose, I pushed the box to the end of the bed, got on the ground and tried to lift it off. It was so heavy I almost dropped it.

Staggering under its weight, I made my way to the brick building, wondering what could be inside the box, and wondering if I could make it go off by shaking it. But then, if that were so, why wouldn't the vibrations of the truck make whatever was in the box go off? Milk went off, so did fish, but this was too heavy to be either. I eased the box onto the ground and waited.

Buckham came out seconds later. He walked past me with merely a nod and pulled the door to the little building open. The building, already small, had such thick sides that the interior was about the size of a phone booth. He hefted the box as if it were empty and set it on a shelf. Then he popped the top off. Inside were sticks of dynamite.

"What the—" I said, before clapping my hands over my mouth.

"Got some stumps need removing," Buckham said, taking a roll of fuse and an old-fashioned cigarette lighter from one of the shelves. "These'll do the trick. Can't buy them for love nor money these days. Anything that goes 'boom' has been commandeered by the military. Had to borrow this from a friend in Shrewton."

He took out four sticks and shoved them in the pocket of his overalls.

"Grab a pick and rake," he said, pointing to another small building. Then he set off.

I caught up with him in a large field behind a stone

barn, after following the path he had made through the brambles and knee-high grass. He was standing by a big stump with an axe stuck in it.

"Me and my boy cut these trees three year ago," he said, sweeping his hand at a row of similar stumps, but without axes. "They need clearing if I'm to expand the field."

The stumps were in a cleared area next to a large field planted half with grain and half with corn.

"Only crops I can make a living with," Buckham said, when he saw me looking. "Corn and barley. Sell it on to whisky makers. Some legal, some maybe not so legal, but where's the harm, eh?"

I shrugged and smiled, feeling as stupid as he probably thought I was.

"Government says if I can prove I have enough arable land, they'll help me buy a tractor. Then they'll buy what I grow, provided I grow what they tell me. That'll be better, and safer, money." He wrenched the axe out of the stump and tossed it on the ground. "I need these gone, but it'd take six men and a horse to pull them out. So, we need a little help."

I nodded, as if I understood.

"Dig a hole under the stump, between the roots. Once you hit soft earth, you can ram the rake end in. That'll be big enough. Make sure it goes under the stump, you ken?"

I laid the rake aside and started swinging the pick. The ground was dry and stony, making it hard going. He left me to it and went to the next stump, where he laid out the dynamite. I dug down until the dirt turned a darker brown, which the pick sank easily into. I got the rake and jammed the handle into the soft earth to make a tunnel angling under the stump. Buckham just

189

watched me, and when he decided I'd done enough, he came back.

"It'll do," he said. Then he took a jackknife out of his pocket and cut a small length of fuse. He must have seen the concern on my face because he said, "It's a slow-burning fuse. This'll give us five minutes to get away. That'll be plenty of time." He stuck the fuse into the end of one of the sticks of dynamite and laid it in the hole I had dug.

He lit the fuse with the lighter, and it sparked to life, hissing and smoking. Using a twig, he pushed the dynamite, and the fuse, into the hole. Then he searched for a longer twig and pushed it farther in, while I started sweating and doing all I could not to scream and run away.

"That should do," he said, standing and wiping his hands on his overalls. "Gather up them tools."

I grabbed the rake and the pick and the axe and followed him as he sauntered to the next stump. There, he put the other sticks back in his pocket and continued his leisurely pace to the next stump. He sat on it, pulled a pouch of tobacco and a small piece of paper from his pocket, and began rolling a cigarette. He lit it with the lighter, took a deep drag and blew the smoke out, staring towards the first stump. I dropped the tools and stood behind him.

The explosion was so loud it hurt my ears. Dirt, rocks, and dust shot into the air like a geyser, and shards of wood rained down. Buckham sat, calmly smoking, watching until the dust settled. Then he nodded and smiled. "Yes, that'll do nicely," he said, rising from the stump. "Let's us get some lunch, see what that sister of yours has fixed up. You can finish the rest this afternoon."

The house was cool and dark, lit only by the light coming through the dusty windows. We sat in a large kitchen at a spacious wooden table, dark with age and numerous stains. Emma had set out some bread and cheese. There was only water to drink, which she got from a hand-pump at the kitchen sink. She'd pulled her hair back and wore an apron that she must have found somewhere. Bowls, pots, and various ingredients sat on the counter, and leaning in the corner was an old shotgun. Set against the far wall was a big black oven that I could feel the heat from, and smell something tasty cooking. I hoped that meant dinner was going to be better than lunch. The bread was stale, and the cheese looked like she had cut mouldy bits off it, but it was food, and I was hungry so I wolfed down what I could.

Emma talked while she ate, complimenting Buckham on the farm and telling him how grateful we were for his kindness. Buckham beamed and looked at her a little too much, but I figured that was a good thing. Appearing friendly was important, especially as I wasn't the best of company.

"That sister of yours is a dab hand in the kitchen," Buckham said as we went back outside.

I nodded. "Yes, she is," I said, hoping it didn't give my accent away.

"You'll be fine with the rest of those stump, eh? Just do like I showed you, then pile the wood chips up and burn them and fill the holes best you can. Don't worry if they aren't level. Plough'll take care of that once I get my tractor."

We crossed the farmyard, heading back to the field but Buckham turned away, towards another outbuilding. A newer structure, made of wood, with a flat, sloping roof. "Got some work to do up here," he said. "Improvements to be made if I'm going to impress the Government men. Got electric in back in thirty-six, but the nearest phone's in Warminster. Not sure they'll mind that. Phone's not required for a tractor. Now you get on." He pulled the lighter from his pocket and tossed it to me. "You'll do fine without me."

"Right-o," I said, cringing at my attempt to speak British English.

Blowing up the stumps was fun, and easy. The rest was not. I spent the afternoon raking up hunks of wood and piling them up so I could set them on fire. Then I raked dirt from all over, trying to get enough to fill the holes. The strip of land with the stumps had been cleared, but not recently, and new weeds had sprouted, some as high as my knees. Raking meant pulling the weeds out, so I piled them on the fire, which made it smoke so badly my eyes stung and my throat went raw. Then I had to scratch around in the brambles for dry wood to throw on top to make the fire flare up again. Despite the dynamite, there were still some stubborn roots that I needed to chop out with the axe before scraping what loose earth I could into the holes. After I tamped them down, they weren't level, but it was the best I could do. It was back-breaking work and by the time the sun was low I was covered in dirt, soot and sweat.

I didn't mind being left alone all afternoon. At least it kept me from having to pretend I was English. After I finished, Buckham didn't come back for me, so I gathered up the tools and made my way to the farmyard.

Buckham was still working on the big shed. He'd

strung a wire from the house to the shed and was busy bolting hinges on the door. The wire sagged over the farmyard and was attached to the shed just below the roof line. It seemed an odd thing to do, but it was his farm and I figured he knew what he was doing.

I hung the rake, shovel, and axe from hooks in the tool shed, then put the lighter and left over fuse in the brick phone booth with the rest of the dynamite. I was sticky with sweat and smelled like smoke and wanted nothing more than a shower, but then I heard Buckham come up behind me.

"All done, then?"

"Yes, sir," I said.

"Then let's go see what your sister has cooked up for us."

The kitchen was warm and filled with the aroma of stew. The counters, visible in the dim light cast by a ceiling lamp, were now empty and clean, and there was only a single, large pot on the stove. Then I noticed the shotgun was no longer there.

Emma served us, and pumped more water for us to drink. Her hair was looser now. Strands stuck out and her brow was shiny with sweat. We didn't talk much. We were too tired for conversation and too hungry to force any. The stew was good, no meat but plenty of potatoes, carrots, and beans. It was tasty and took the edge off my hunger.

"I think it's time we all turned in," Buckham said, leering at Emma as she cleared the plates. "I'm afraid I can't offer the best accommodation, but it will be better than what you'da had if you were still walking."

"I only have two bedrooms upstairs, you understand," Buckham said as Emma carried the dishes to the sink. He had turned to look at me, and I noticed Emma—when she saw Buckham was no longer staring at her—pull a drawer open and slip a paring knife into her pocket. "There's mine," Buckham continued, "and my boy's. I haven't been in his room since he left. I want him to come back and find it just the way it was, and I'm a bit sentimental about that. But I've fixed you up a nice little bedroom outside. You'll be fine there."

I felt a nervousness rising in my stomach and, looking at Emma, could see she felt it too. But we didn't have a choice, so we got our packs and followed Buckham outside. He switched on an outside light that bathed the farmyard in harsh, yellow light, and more light spilled out of the open doorway of the big shed he'd been working on. We walked towards it, with Buckham behind. Just outside the door, we stopped. He'd put an electric light inside and we clearly saw a bed of straw with blankets and pillows on it. It was not uninviting, but something didn't feel right. I thought about the house, and his story about the two bedrooms. The downstairs had a large kitchen, a big living room, a dining room, and a hallway with a staircase leading up. There had to be at least three, possibly four bedrooms in the house.

I looked at Emma. Her eyes were wide. She put her hand in her pocket for the knife. Then I heard the truck door open and close and two metallic clicks. I looked behind me and saw Buckham walking towards the shed, the shotgun in his hands, pointing at us.

"You didn't think your pathetic attempt at hiding your accent fooled me, did you? You're the ones they're looking for." He motioned with the shotgun, urging us to go into the shed. "I've made you a nice little nest in there," he said, "so I would appreciate it if you'd step inside."

Emma sighed and bowed her head. There was no, "you go this way and I'll go that way." Buckham could kill us both twice over with the shotgun, and a paring knife was no use against it.

"Don't try anything heroic now," Buckham said to me, stepping closer. "The man said he only wanted you. This girl," he said, waving the shotgun at Emma, "is no sister of yours, but that's no never mind to me. I'll get money for you, and she'll certainly sweeten the deal, so I don't want to have to shoot her. I will, though, if you try anything stupid. So, step lively now. In you get."

There was nothing we could do. Emma stepped through the door, and I followed. Moments later the door slammed. I heard the latch click, then a padlock snapped closed.

Chapter 35

Mitch

If it had been a different night, we'd have had quite a party.

After putting the base back into the best shape we could, and checking over our Spitfires, we had dinner in the Officers' Mess and retired to the Officers' Club, where we were to bed down for the night. Tables were pushed aside, and cots were brought in and made up with blankets and pillows while the pilots sat on the other side of the room, drinking, smoking, and watching. But there were no jokes about not having far to stumble to bed. There were no jokes at all. We were tired and unnerved by the destruction visited on the base. And beyond that, we all knew that the raid was a harbinger of the main attack to come.

"To a job well done," James said, clinking his glass to mine. In the subdued atmosphere, it sounded jarring. "The runway is back in top form. No one will be left behind tomorrow."

The other pilots mumbled in agreement, but they stared into their beer, each lost in his own thoughts.

Once repairs were under way and some of the wreckage had been cleared, we were allowed into what was left of the barracks. Most of it was destroyed, but some of the men managed to salvage a few personal items. I had been luckiest of all. Charlie and I had the bunks near the stone portion of the walls, so our foot lockers were hardly damaged. I'd had them brought to the club and both were now at the foot of my cot.

"Do you think it will be tomorrow, Chief?" Ronnie Folds, the one they called Ditter, asked.

Chief, who also answered to Flight Leader Brian Kingcombe, nodded. "They've been pushing harder and harder for some weeks now. No reason to believe they won't turn the full force of the Luftwaffe on us sooner or later. Sooner would be my guess."

Ziggy drained his glass and banged it down on the table. "Did you see those Stukas? Flying in here like they owned the place? And there were only a dozen of them. What are we going to do when there's a hundred?"

"Or a thousand," Bugs added.

I sat with my hands wrapped around my glass, staring into it, like the others. They probably thought I was mulling over the same things they were, but I was pretty sure I wasn't. I wanted to tell them they would win, but I couldn't be sure. Not yet. That was up to Charlie, and I had the feeling he had not yet completed his task. So, winning or losing was still up for grabs.

And even if they won, many men would die.

It reminded me of the night before the Battle of Camlann, with the soldiers sitting around the campfire, thinking about the next day, the way soldiers from time immemorial had done. The same way we were now.

The pilots were scared, I was scared, but when the call came, they would answer, and that was why—

197

certain as I was that things were going to get very bad very soon—I wouldn't have traded places with anyone.

The low talk continued, mixed with occasional bravado. Fulbright joined us, but all he had to offer was confirmation that something big was up. No one felt much like drinking after that and we silently drifted to our new, hopefully temporary, bunks. With my uniform folded and tucked under my bed, I got ready to face the long night. Soon the dark hall, still smelling of stale beer and pipe smoke, settled into the sounds of heavy breathing punctuated by the occasional snore.

"Gunner," James whispered from the cot next to me, "you awake?"

"Yeah."

"What do you think?"

"About what?"

"About what's coming. Do you think, you know, it's going to be all right?"

I thought about this for a while.

"It will," I said. "These pilots, all of them, not just the one eight eight, but all of them, at Tangmere, Biggin Hill and the others, will be heroes. You'll be praised for your bravery and raised as high in the nation's esteem as the Knights of King Arthur's court. You will become legends, and you will win."

I stopped then and waited but James said nothing. All I heard were the sounds of slumber. I rolled to my side waiting for sleep to take me, and whispered to no one but myself, "As long as Charlie gets to the Tor in time."

Chapter 36

Charlie

Emma threw her pack at the blankets and kicked the straw. "Shit," she said. Then she said things I had never heard a girl say before, and some things I had never heard anyone say before. I dropped my own pack and tried the door, even though I knew it was useless. Buckham had turned the door around, putting the handle inside and the hinges outside, fastening them with smooth-headed bolts so there was no chance of getting out.

I put my eye to a seam between the boards. I could see light, but nothing else.

"Give me the knife," I said.

Emma stopped and took a couple of breaths. After she calmed herself down, she dug the knife out of her pocket and handed it to me.

"Do you think you can cut through the door with it?"

"No," I said, "but I might be able to see what he's up to."

I stuck the short blade into the seam and moved it up and down. It opened the crack enough that I could see a sliver of the farmyard.

"He's not out there," I said. Then I saw him, coming out of the house, without the shotgun. "He's getting in his truck."

After that, I didn't need to see. I heard the truck start. The engine whined and then the sound faded as he drove away.

"Where's he going?" Emma asked.

"Warminster," I said. "That's where the nearest phone is. He's going to call Farber."

"We need to get out of here."

I checked the walls. The shed had been recently built, so the boards were hardly weathered, much less rotten. The only spot that looked promising was the far corner. There, the wall sat on the ground and moisture had seeped into the wood. It hadn't made much difference, but it was the only chance we had.

I cut a vertical line in the board. It was hard wood, but softened just enough that I could make a groove. I dug at it harder and snapped the blade. At first, I felt a wave of hopelessness wash over me, but then I found that the short stump of metal that remained was even better for scraping at the board. I dug as quickly as I could, making a shallow V in the wood. Then I kicked it. It didn't budge. I kicked again and again. Nothing.

I inspected the groove I had made and discovered the walls were built of overlapping boards, like shingles. The board I cut was held in place by the one above, and that one by the one above it. I couldn't kick it in half unless I broke the boards above it. To break the bottom board, I'd have to cut a horizontal line, as well as a vertical line, and make them both deeper than the cut I had already made.

"How long do you think we have?" Emma asked, when she saw how much needed to be done.

"I don't know. I'll just have to do what I can and hope I have enough time."

"We could stall them," she said. "If they can't get in, we'll have more time to get out."

I stopped scraping at the board and looked up at her. "What do you mean?"

"Come help me."

She led me to the front of the shed. "If we can tie the door handle, they won't be able to open it."

I nodded. "Yeah, but with what?"

She pointed to the light, dangling from an electric wire that rose to the ceiling and out of the shed near the roof. The light was too high to reach, unless one of us held the other up.

"The trick," she said, "will be to avoid getting electrocuted."

We got one of the blankets and I squatted down to let Emma get on my shoulders. Then I stood up, bracing myself against the wall. Emma reached high, wrapped the blanket around the light fixture and gripped it tight.

"I have it," she said, and I ducked, leaving her hanging in the air.

Whatever had been holding the wire gave way. I heard a pop and saw a flash, and everything went dark. Emma landed next to me with a thud, dragging yards of electrical wire with her.

"Get my torch," she said.

It was pitch dark in the shed, not even a sliver of light leaked in through the slit I had made in the door, so I had to feel my way to where she'd left her pack.

"I'll tie it to the handle and thread it around this upright," she said when we could see again. "There's enough here to loop it ten or twelve times, then I'll tie it off tight. That will slow them down a little."

I wondered how long that might be, and didn't

want to remind her that Buckham had an axe, and other tools, that could make short work of the door. Instead, I looked through the slit to see why no light was getting in.

"It's dark out there," I said. "He left the outside light on. What happened to it?"

"We must have blown the fuse," Emma said, feeding the wire from the door handle through the gap between the upright and the wall. "That could work to our advantage, as well."

I went back to the corner. It was dark, but the glow of her flashlight gave me enough light to continue. When she was done, Emma came to me, carrying her flashlight and both packs.

"As soon as you break through, get away. Throw your pack through the hole and get out. I'll follow."

I nodded and kept scratching at the board. It was hard work. Each pass cut a minuscule amount of wood away. I scraped and scraped until my hands were raw. Then I kicked, hoping it would break, or at least give a little. It never did. I cut away at the board for what seemed like an hour, then I kept cutting. When the V became as deep as the metal sticking out of the knife handle, I made the V wider. And still the board remained stubbornly in place.

When another hour or so went by, we heard the truck again.

"He's coming back," Emma said.

I kept scraping at the board as Emma went to the door and looked through the slit.

"Buckham's getting out. There's someone following him."

I heard a car door slam.

"It's Farber. They're coming this way."

202

I dropped the knife, scooted back, and kicked at the board. Nothing.

We waited, holding our breath. The padlock clicked open. The door rattled.

I heard Buckham swear, then he said, "What the …?"

"Are you sure they're in there?" Farber's voice.

"They're in there all right." A boom as Buckham kicked the door. "They've jammed it somehow."

"Well, find a way to unjam it."

I readied myself to kick again but Emma stopped me.

"He'll hear," she said. "He'll know what we're up to and come around to this side."

"Then what do we do."

She held a finger to her lips. "Just wait."

A few seconds later a boom shattered the silence.

"He's got an axe," I said.

"Now," Emma said.

We both kicked at the board, our efforts covered by the sound of Buckham battering at the door with the axe. We kicked and kicked again. The axe hit the door. Wood splintered. The axe hit again.

"Harder," Emma said.

We both kicked with all our strength. The board cracked and bowed outward.

"Again!"

The board broke, but the hole wasn't big enough.

The axe broke through. Another swing. The sound was hollow this time, and I knew he'd broken through.

We kicked at the pieces of board to open the hole wider.

"Almost there."

Frantic hammering as Buckham chopped away at the latch. Then the door banged open.

Emma shoved my pack through the hole. "Get out," she said, grabbing her own pack and the flashlight. "I'll stall them."

"But—"

"You've got to get away."

She ran towards the door. Buckham was already inside with Farber right behind him. Emma charged and swung her pack. Buckham ducked and the pack hit Farber in the face. Then she brought the flashlight down on the back of Buckham's head. The flashlight shattered. The shed went dark.

In that instant, I felt an aching in my chest as if my heart might burst. She was the bravest person I had ever known, and I was the most cowardly, because I was about to abandon her.

Scuffling in the dark. Emma shrieked. "Get away! Get away!"

I knew she wasn't shouting at Farber or Buckham, she was telling me to go.

I dived for the hole and squirmed through. A hand grabbed for my foot. I kicked it off and dragged myself farther out. I was almost free. Then a hand with an iron grip wrapped around my ankle. I dug at the ground to pull myself forward but the hand held tight, pulling me back into the shed. I flipped onto my back and saw the hand and the muscular forearm and knew it was Buckham. I raised my other leg and brought my heel down on my ankle. It hurt, but not as much as it hurt Buckham. He grunted. His grip loosened and I pulled free.

Scooping up my pack, I ran into the darkness, leaving Emma behind.

I ran as fast as I could and hid behind one of the outbuildings. There, I tried to steady myself and calm my pounding heart. I peeked around the building, watching, waiting.

Soon, three figures emerged from the shed. Farber, and Buckham, holding Emma's hands behind her back. They went across the farmyard and entered the house. A flickering light told me they had lit a lantern. I waited, trying to come up with a plan. Then Farber stepped out the door, holding the lantern high. Light pooled around him as he scanned the darkness.

"It seems we're at an impasse," he said. "You're free, and you can scuttle away with what I want, but I think I have something you want. So, I'm willing to make a deal. The girl for the Talisman. You have five minutes to decide, or I'll start giving the girl to you one piece at a time."

He went back into the house. The door slammed. Emma screamed again.

She'd sacrificed herself so I could escape, but I wasn't going to leave without rescuing her. The question was: how?

I leaned against the wall out of sight of the house, my mind whirling. What advantage did I have? There must be something. Then it hit me. Farber didn't really know what the Talisman looked like. He'd only seen it for a few seconds and in the dark any black stone would do.

Problem was, there weren't any stones that looked like the Talisman. I couldn't search in the farmyard, so I felt around the base of the building, then I went to another one, where the dynamite was kept. I still didn't find one, but a new idea came to me. I pulled the door open, took a stick of dynamite, the lighter and the fuse, and ran back to the shed.

I placed the dynamite behind the shed and reeled off about fifteen minutes worth of fuse. I had no knife, so I had to bite through it, which wasn't easy. And it tasted foul. When I was done. I shoved the end of the fuse into the dynamite and lit it.

"Your time is almost up," Farber shouted. His voice startled me, and I began to panic. I moved as swiftly and silently as I could, away from the shed, and started shouting back as I moved.

"All right," I said. "But we'll do it my way. I'll tell you where the Talisman is. You release Emma."

As soon as I stopped, I moved again, behind another building. There, I left my pack, and moved on.

"I keep the girl until I have the Talisman," he said, looking to where I had been. "Then I'll release you both."

Fact chance, I thought. He would kill us as soon as the Talisman was in his hand.

"Bring the Talisman to me," he said, "unless you want your girlfriend to lose a finger."

"I don't have it," I said. "I hid it. It's inside the shed where Buckham held us, hidden under the straw next to the back wall."

I could see this going wrong. He'd tell me to fetch it and I'd tell him I wouldn't, and he'd threaten Emma and all the while the clock was ticking, and the fuse was burning. But he didn't do that. Instead, he went back inside. Then Emma came out, with Farber following her, holding the lantern in one hand and a gun—pointed at Emma's back—in the other. The blood drained from my face. What do I do now?

I watched until they entered the shed, then I left

my hiding place and went towards the shed. Could I surprise him? It might work if I had a weapon. I wondered where the axe that Buckham had used to bash through the door was. Then I wondered where he was, and a familiar metallic click sounded behind me.

"Let's go," he said, pushing the cold muzzle of the shotgun into the back of my neck. "Nice and slow. No funny business."

I walked into the shed, with Buckham behind me. Emma was going through the straw at the back of the shed, near where I had placed the dynamite. Farber stood next to her, holding the lantern, and his pistol. He smiled as we came in.

"Well, isn't this a pleasant surprise?"

It pleased me to see that he still had the bandage on his head and moved with a slight limp. He waved the pistol at Emma. "You, go join your boyfriend." Then to Buckham he said, "They move. Shoot them."

He tucked the gun into a holster inside his jacket and started searching through the straw. How long had it been? Ten minutes at least, maybe more? How accurate was the fuse? How much did I actually use?

I took Emma's hand and pulled her back. Buckham jammed the shotgun into my back. "That's enough of that. He's said I could shoot you, and I will. I'll save the girl for later, though."

I spun around, away from the business end of the shotgun, and grabbed the barrel. The blast nearly knocked me off my feet. A hole appeared in the back wall, five feet from Farber, who jumped back, dropping the lantern. It broke open and the straw flared up. Then he fumbled for his gun.

My hands burned and smoke filled the air.

Buckham yanked at the shotgun, but I held fast. He still had his finger on the trigger, but he couldn't fire, or he might hit Farber. I twisted the barrel, bending his finger. He yelped, so I twisted harder and heard a snap.

Buckham yowled and I pulled the shotgun from him, swung it around and smacked him in the head with the stock. He fell like a sack of potatoes.

"Look out!"

It was Emma. She slammed into me, pushing us both to the floor as a shot rang out. I pulled the shotgun around and fired a wild shot in Farber's direction. It missed, but hit the wall next to him.

Before he could recover, I jumped up, pulling Emma with me, and dived for the door.

The explosion threw us both to the ground. Wood, straw, and dirt scoured my back and a hurricane of heat blasted over me. The world went white, then yellow and the stench of gunpowder mixed with the smell of smoke. I lifted my head and my vision wavered. I felt as if I was underwater, where everything was in slow motion and strangely silent. I struggled to my knees and tried to pull Emma up. Her eyes were wide but unfocused.

"Are you all right?"

I spoke the words but heard nothing.

"Are you alright?" I screamed, so loud it made my throat raw, but no sound came out.

Emma blinked. Her lips moved. The silence remained.

I stood up and helped Emma to her feet and we staggered from the shed. Yellow light from the flames flickered across the farmyard. I saw Farber's car, and Buckham's truck.

"Wait here," I said. Emma looked at me, but I could tell she didn't hear. I left her and went back into the burning shed. Buckham was still lying where he fell. I grabbed a leg and began to pull. Then Emma was beside me. Her mouth opened and closed. It looked like she was asking what I was doing. I shook my head and kept pulling. She grabbed his other leg and together we got him into the farmyard. Then I went through his pockets and pulled out his truck keys. I held them up and jiggled them in front of Emma, then pointed to the truck. She nodded and staggered towards it.

I went as fast as I could to get my pack. It was hard as my legs were unsteady and a ringing, like the sound of a million bees, filled my head. As I wavered towards the truck, the sound of crackling and popping from the burning shed came to me. The ringing was still there, but I could hear. Faintly. Emma was standing by the truck, waiting for me.

"Get in," I shouted. My voice sounded like it came through a wad of cotton.

Emma got in the passenger's side. I opened the driver's door, threw my pack inside and climbed in.

I fumbled the key into the ignition and turned it. The truck bucked and stopped. I looked at Emma, puzzled.

"Push the clutch," she said, her voice coming as if from a distance away.

"What?"

"The clutch, that pedal there."

I pushed it in. The truck started. I revved the engine. Nothing happened.

"Let the clutch out," Emma said.

I did. The truck lurched forward and stopped. The

silence returned and I thought my hearing had gone again. Then I realized that the truck had stalled.

"Don't you know how to drive?" Emma asked.

"Well, yes, but not with a clutch."

Something bumped into the truck. I looked out the window and saw Buckham's face two inches from mine.

"He's trying to get in," Emma shouted. "Lock the door."

I ran my hand over the armrest, looking for the lock. Emma dived across me and pushed a button on the door as Buckham yanked on the handle. Emma locked her own door as Buckham pounded on the window with his fist. Then he left, walking back towards the burning shed.

"What's he doing?" Emma asked.

Buckham bent and picked something off the ground. Then he turned back towards us.

"He's got the axe."

"Quick. Switch places."

She scrambled over top of me, and I squirmed under her into the passenger's seat. Buckham was nearly on us.

Emma started the truck and jammed the gearshift. The truck made a grinding sound, then we shot forward. Buckham swung the axe. It glanced off the door frame. Emma cranked the wheel and made a tight circle. The truck went up on two wheels and we barely missed another outbuilding. Then she straightened up and headed towards Buckham,

She pressed the accelerator. The truck's engine whined, and we sped forward. She pulled a knob on the dashboard and the headlights came on, pinning Buckham in white light. He threw the axe and dived

210

to the side. The axe skittered up the hood, hit the windshield and bounced over the roof, leaving a big star in the glass.

Emma jammed the gearshift again and gained more speed. We headed down the long driveway, away from the farm, towards the road that would lead us to the Tor.

Chapter 37

Mitch

The lights came on, blinding me. I sat up and blinked. The clock on the wall said four in the morning.

"Come on, men," Fulbright called. "You're due at dispersal at oh four thirty."

A chorus of moans and groans filled the room, but one by one we got up and, still in our underwear, made our way to the temporary wash basins that had been set up for us. I had to wait in line, but it didn't take long. I scrubbed myself with cold water, dressed in my uniform and headed with the others to the Officers' Mess.

The world was quiet and still and dark as we strolled across the grass. The cool morning air revived me and by the time I reached the mess I was properly awake.

We wolfed down toast and bacon and drank cups of tea. There was little conversation. Even James, sitting next to me, hadn't much to say. It seemed as if we'd hardly sat down when Fulbright stood up.

"All right, men, let's go."

The squadron rose, some still stuffing toast in their mouths. Chairs scraped the floor, forks landed on plates, and we shuffled for the door.

Behind us, Fulbright continued. "Come on,

Edridge, get the skids under you. And Holmes, put some bacon in your pocket if you're that hungry."

We wandered across the runway to the dispersal hut. I found it strangely comforting. I had only been flying a few times, and had never been on an actual mission, but it seemed a familiar routine. There was a flight board which listed the "Order of Battle." Fulbright was flying with us, so we would be at full strength. He was Red One, James was Red Two, and I was Red Three. And that was fine with me.

Then I went to my locker and put on my flying kit, making sure to wrap the silk scarf around my neck. When I finished putting on my Sidcot suit and boots, I slung my parachute over my shoulder and headed for the door. James walked beside me as we made our way to the Spitfires, which were being tuned up by the mechanics.

One by one they started up, shattering the morning stillness with the roar of their engines. Flames shot from exhaust pipes and smoke swirled through the still air. Behind the planes, wind from the propellers kicked up dust and laid the grass flat. As I approached, I felt the ground vibrate under my feet as the Spitfires strained to be released. It was an awe-inspiring sight, and my heart might have burst with wonder and gratitude if it wasn't for the niggling thought that many of us might not see the end of the day.

I went to my plane. Roddis was in the cockpit, making adjustments. He gave me a thumbs-up and I returned it. Then I hung my parachute on the port wing, like James had told me to. It would keep me from having to drag it around all morning; I could put it on when we were scrambled.

The engine roared louder as Roddis performed the final tests, then it sputtered and stopped. Roddis climbed out onto the wing, gave me another thumbs up, and jumped to the ground. I climbed up and looked into the cockpit. All seemed ready. I hung my helmet on the stick and plugged in the radio and oxygen. There was nothing to do after that except return to the dispersal hut and wait.

James and I walked back together. When we got there, he handed me a life jacket.

"Here," he said. "Put your Mae West on."

"My what?"

I pulled it over my head and James helped me fasten the straps. "Mae West, she's an American actress. Well proportioned, understand?"

I nodded, pretending I did. We sat and waited.

That was the hardest part. The call could come at any second, or it might be hours, or it might not come at all. The pilots read, napped, and smoked, but there was little conversation. Everyone was intent on his own thoughts, and none of them looked particularly happy.

When the phone rang, twelve heads shot up. The telephone orderly lifted the handset.

"Yes, sir," he said. "One eight eight squadron now at readiness. Twelve aircraft. Right, sir."

Then he hung up, and twelve heads bowed back down.

I wished I had brought a book with me. There was nothing to do and James didn't feel like talking. To tell the truth, neither did I, so I watched the clock, playing a game with myself to see if I could not look at it for five straight minutes. I kept losing.

Then the phone rang again. The orderly picked it

up and listened. "Understood." He put the handset down. "Squadron scramble. Full strength."

Twelve men raced for the door. I squeezed through and ran to my Spitfire, my heart pounding. It wasn't far, but I was already out of breath by the time I got there. Roddis was in the cockpit, starting the engine. I put on my parachute and climbed onto the wing. Roddis got out and helped me in, strapping my harness for me as I put on my helmet. He patted me on the shoulder and then was gone.

The Spitfires pulled out, Black Section first, then Green, then Yellow. Red Section, led by Fulbright, taxied last. James followed, and I trailed behind him.

By the time we were in position, Black and Green were airborne, and Yellow was forming up. We pulled in behind them, Fulbright in front, James off his port wing and me on the starboard.

The radio crackled in my ear, and I heard Fulbright's voice. "Ready, men. Here we go."

I released the brakes and heard the hiss of escaping air. Then I eased the throttle open, moving in unison with Red One. I touched the rudder to correct my course, keeping the Spitfire straight and in formation as we rumbled down the runway after Yellow. I kept Fulbright's wing in sight, trying to maintain my distance.

The Spitfire bumped and bounced over the grass. I gave it more throttle. The tail came up, and with one more bump I rose into the air and flew over the perimeter fence, my eyes locked on Red One. Once in the air we quickly formed up: twelve Spitfires, four sections, two flights—the full squadron, heading into battle. I looked over my port wing at James and saw the sun peeking over the horizon.

"Come on, Charlie," I said aloud, my voice barely audible over the roar of the engine. "Please, get it done."

Chapter 38

Charlie

It was just starting to get light when we first saw the Tor.

Emma drove like a madwoman for a while, until I convinced her no one was after us. Then she started paying attention to the roads and taking us in what she hoped was a westerly direction. Occasionally, we travelled on modern, wide highways, but mostly we trundled along on roads so narrow I thought she might have driven onto a pathway by mistake. It was frustrating in the darkness, turning corners, hitting dead ends, doubling back.

At last, we found Shepton Mallet and, from there, we took narrower and narrower back roads until I was certain we were hopelessly lost. Then, as the sky began to lighten, and Emma left the narrow lane we were on to drive down an even narrower lane, I saw in the distance a dark shape rising above the brightening horizon.

"That's it," I said, my voice rising in excitement. "That's the Tor."

The lane we were on—so narrow the weeds rustled against the sides of the truck—pointed directly at it, so that it loomed larger and larger through the cracked windshield as Emma drove, faster than was comfortable, down the track. Then the road ended suddenly in a T junction, and she nearly drove straight through a wooden gate. She slammed on the brakes, and we ended up sideways in the road.

"Pull over," I said. "We can walk from here."

Emma ground the gears, backed the truck into the narrow lane we had been on, then hit the accelerator. The truck streaked forward and crashed through the gate.

"What are you doing?"

The truck bounced and thudded over the grassy field. I looked around to see if there were any angry bulls or farmers in it.

"Faster this way," Emma said, grimly gripping the wheel and peering through the windshield.

She drove to the edge of the Tor and parked at the base of the incline.

"Let's go," she said, jumping out of the truck.

I grabbed my pack and followed.

"It's so different now," I said. "When I was here last, it was in the middle of a lake, and in 1066 we had to navigate through a swamp to get here."

"Are you sure we're in the right place?"

I started climbing. "I'm sure. The hill itself looks the same, it's just the land around it."

From where I was, I saw fields, then the road, woods, and more fields. The Tor still had remnants of the path, but there were no bushes growing on them. We climbed to the first level, then the next and the next.

Emma followed, looking bewildered. "What are we searching for?"

"The entrance to the temple."

"There's a temple here?"

"Inside," I said. "There's a secret door I have to

218

open. It's on the fifth level."

We climbed to the next level, and then up to the fifth. Then we sat to catch our breath.

Emma looked down the grassy slope. "What are the levels for?"

"They were paths, originally, with big bushes growing on the sides of them. You couldn't climb up like we did, you had to walk the maze to get to the top of the Tor."

"Isn't the temple at the top?"

"No." I got up and started searching along the slope. "It's on this level. Somewhere along here there's a big white rock. That's where the entrance is."

Emma got up and helped me look. "Are you sure it's still here?"

"It was really big. It wasn't going anywhere. It must still be here."

We looked, but all we found was grass.

"It must be grown over," Emma said. "How are we going to find it?"

"It can't be. It was too big for that. It's got to be here somewhere."

We worked our way along the ridge, covering every inch. Then we went the other way and found nothing.

I sat, exhausted, leaning against the side of the Tor. Emma came and sat beside me.

"Maybe we're on the wrong level," she said. "Are you sure it was on this one?"

"Believe me, we counted carefully. It was the fifth level, I am certain."

Even so, I looked to the next level down, number four, and to the one after that, and after that, until I got to the truck, sitting at the base of the hill, with the sun glinting off its windshield.

"Yup, this is number five, and … wait a minute." I looked at the rising sun. "That's east," I said, pointing.

Emma nodded. "Yes, that's usually where the sun comes up."

"Then this is the north side. The door is on the south side. Come on."

We ran around the Tor, following the pathway. On the other side, with renewed optimism, we searched again, and again found nothing. Disgusted and tired, I sat, with my elbows on my knees, supporting my chin with my fist.

From this side, a farm track ran close to the base of the Tor. Beyond that were fields and houses. I looked down at the fields that had once been a lake, then to the first level, the second, and the third.

"We're on the fourth level," I said. "We have to go up one more."

We scrambled up the slope and searched again. This time, Emma saw something white lying against the side of the hill. "It that it?"

We ran towards it.

"Yes," I said. "That's it."

When we got to it, I dropped my pack and leaned on the stone, breathing hard.

"That's not big," Emma said. "It's huge."

It was. Large and egg-shaped, and different from anything else on the Tor.

"The entrance is here," I said. "And the stone opens the door. But only a Guardian wearing Arthur's cloak can turn it."

I opened my pack, pulled the cloak out, and put it on.

Emma stared at me. "Arthur's cloak?"

I nodded, then looked at the not-so-distant houses. When I'd been here before, there was nothing around. Now, someone might see us, but we'd have to take the chance. I put my hand on the stone like Mitch had done.

Emma stood beside me. "What are you doing?"

I concentrated on the rock. Mitch had done it, so I knew I could. Or at least I thought I could.

"I need to turn it."

Emma shook her head. "That's impossible."

I turned to look at her, trying to view these incredible happenings through her eyes.

"You've heard some pretty strange things from me," I said, "and you've said you believe them."

Emma nodded. "I do. At least, I think I do."

"It's a lot to take on. And all you have is my word. I understand."

Emma stepped close and put her arms around my shoulders. "I'm not saying I doubt you, but ..."

I put a finger on her lips. "I just want you to be ready. From here on, you won't be able to doubt; you will be cursed with knowledge, and your ability to believe the unbelievable is going to be put to a severe test."

I turned my eyes back to the rock and laid my hand on the side, like Mitch had done. At first, a hopelessness began to bloom in my chest, but then a sense of calm descended. I took a breath and pushed. The rock rotated, and the ground began to rumble.

Emma jumped back. I grabbed her arm to keep her from tumbling down the slope. Next to the rock, a vertical slit appeared. Dirt and stones tumbled to the ground as the split yawned, exposing the top of the stairway. Emma's eyes grew wide, and her jaw dropped. I picked up my pack. "That's the door. Let's go."

Still wearing the cloak, I went through the opening, pulling Emma by the hand. The stairs were just as I remembered them. We descended and, as before, the walls of the cavern glowed with faint light, enabling us to see. At the base of the stairs Emma gave a yelp.

"There's a skeleton here!"

I kept walking, pulling her with me. "Lubbick," I said. "He's the reason the Talisman isn't here."

We continued along the corridor, heading towards the temple. The air was cool, musty, and melancholy. It was a familiar ache, a shadow of the horrific sorrow, dulled through the centuries. Emma let go of my hand and covered her eyes.

"Why do I feel like crying."

"Don't worry," I said. "You're feeling what the Tor feels. We'll soon make it right."

Then the hallway ended, and we entered the temple. Emma gasped. The room was as awe inspiring as I remembered. So wide and tall the walls and ceiling disappeared into gloom. Several thick columns rose from the floor into the darkness above, and on the far wall, glowing with faint white light, was the altar. It was carved into the side of the temple, not a full sculpture, but a bas-relief depiction of a platform, altar table, and bulky cross decorated with intricate knots and intertwining ropes. At the centre of the cross was a hole, the receptacle of the Talisman, cut into the temple wall.

We walked past the columns, to the middle of the vast room. Emma looked around, her eyes wide, unable to take in what she was seeing.

"What is this place?"

"It's the temple of the Talisman, which is supposed to be in the cross. That unites the power of the Land and the Sky. When I was last here, when we put the Talisman in the cross, the spirits of Arthur's knights came. They sleep here, waiting and watching."

I put my pack down and took the Talisman out. It vibrated in my hand.

"Waiting for what?" Emma asked.

I stood, looking at the cross. "To be called. If the Land is ever in peril, the knights will rise to defend it. But only if the Talisman is in place. And it can only be put into the cross by the hand of someone descended from Arthur. I guess that's why I'm here."

I took a breath. This was what all the other adventures were for. This is what they led to, and why I had come back.

"I guess this is it," I said. "Let's take the Talisman home."

Then a voice came from the back of the room.

"I think not."

I looked. It was Farber, emerging from behind the columns, a pistol in his hand.

"I'll take that now, if it pleases you, and even if it doesn't."

Chapter 39

Mitch

With the wheels pumped up, I throttled to climbing power and settled in, concentrating on holding my position.

Fulbright's voice came over the radio. "Control, this is Roman Leader. One eight eight squadron airborne."

Roman, I had recently been informed, was the squadron's call sign.

Control replied, "Roger, Roman leader."

We continued to climb, twelve Spitfires in formation. It might have been a thrilling sight from the ground, but up here it was magnificent. All of us concentrating on our position, yet ready to pounce as soon as we spotted the enemy. The sky was clear with only a few cirrostratus clouds visible. Not enough to provide cover or to hide a lurking Messerschmitt.

A few minutes later, the radio crackled again.

"Roman leader, this is Control. Two fifty plus approaching Dungeness. Vector to 120. Over"

"Control, this is Roman leader. Message received and understood."

"Roman leader, bandits include many snappers. I say again, many snappers. Keep a good lookout. Over"

"Control, this is Roman. Understood. I am

steering 120 and climbing. Over."

"Okay, Roman."

And that was it. We were on our way to tackle an enemy invasion of over two-hundred and fifty Luftwaffe planes. There would be many bombers, but also snappers, the code name for Messerschmitt 109s.

We climbed hard to ten thousand feet. Then levelled out. Below, the green fields of England gave way to the grey, choppy waters of the Channel. I adjusted my goggles and turned on the oxygen in case I needed it. I might be too busy later. I felt hollow inside. My mouth was dry, and my arms felt heavy. What were we heading for?

The radio crackled again.

"Roman leader, you are very close now."

"Roger, Control, this is Roman leader. I see them. Over."

There were a few moments of silence, then, "Understood, Roman leader. Good luck."

I looked ahead. The sky was vast and blue and apparently empty. Then, in the far distance, I saw tiny black dots, hundreds of them. They grew quickly, and soon it was easy to tell which were the bombers, and which were the Messerschmitts. They spotted us and climbed to gain the advantage. We were a tiny force, no more than a platoon of men attacking a battalion. There would be others, naturally, but even if ten squadrons attacked at full strength, we'd still be outnumbered two to one.

I felt my hand shake on the stick. Then a voice came over the radio. I think it might have been Yo-Yo, who spoke for us all.

"God in heaven," he said, "what have we got ourselves into?"

Chapter 40

Charlie

Farber didn't look good. His suitcoat, shirt and pants were in tatters. His hat, and his bandage were gone, half his hair was burned off and the right side of his face was disfigured by blisters. His right arm hung limply at his side and, when he walked, he dragged his right leg.

The gun was in his left hand, and wobbled as he approached us. He was still too far away to make an accurate shot. Emma must have thought the same thing.

"Run," she said.

We ran towards the nearest column. A shot rang out, echoing through the huge room. We ducked behind the column as a second shot came. It hit the column and speckled the side of my face with stone fragments. We huddled together, out of danger for the moment.

"He's coming this way," Emma said. "He'll kill us if he gets close enough.

"I've got to get to the altar," I said, feeling helpless. There was no way I could do that unless we disarmed Farber. Then Emma grabbed the Talisman out of my hand.

"He's going to go for you," she said. "Distract him, Lead him away. I'll put the Talisman in the cross."

"You?"

"I'm a descendant of Arthur as well. You said that was the requirement."

It was. And Merlin had said that the bloodline of women was stronger than in men. She was right, but I didn't want to let her go.

"It's too dangerous."

She pulled me to her and kissed me. "We've been in danger before. Just go. And don't get shot."

"I'll try not to."

I ran, heading for the next column, slapping my feet on the stone floor, the cloak flapping behind me. Farber turned my way and fired. I paused behind the column, then ran on. A glance over my shoulder confirmed he was tracking me, facing away from where Emma was hiding. I saw her break cover as I dived behind the next column.

I didn't wait long. I ran on, waiting for another shot. None came. I reached the next column, skidded to a stop, and blinked at what I saw there. A sword, old and rusted, was leaning against the stone. Then it all came back to me. It was the sword I had left behind when we'd been here with Merlin. The sword I had seen years earlier, or several hundred years later, and had once again left behind. It was my sword the one I had carried in the battle of Camlann.

The leather scabbard was gone, disintegrated into dust, the metal parts fused to the sword by over a thousand years of rust. It was no longer sharp enough to use as a sword, but it was heavy enough to be a weapon. I picked it up and peeked around the column. No shots came because Farber was no longer looking at me.

Emma had reached the altar. Her feet were already on the platform, and she was climbing to the cross. Farber had seen her and pointed the pistol, struggling to hold it steady. I opened my mouth to shout a warning, but it was too late. Smoke shot from the barrel and a sharp crack shattered the silence. In that instant, with the report of the revolver clapping against my ears, the vision the Talisman had shown me, had cursed me with, the vision I had been struggling to push aside, became clear. And I knew what was going to happen.

My heart sank, and I screamed.

"NOOOOO!"

Emma shuddered and slipped. A red stain bloomed on the side of her jacket. Farber took a shambling step towards her.

Emma steadied herself and climbed higher, her left hand holding the alter, her right stretching up towards the cross. Farber aimed his gun.

I rushed towards him, the sword in my hand.

Farber ignored me and concentrated on holding the pistol steady. I wasn't going to get to him in time. In desperation, I flung the sword as hard as I could. It sailed through the air, end over end, arcing towards him. It hit him in the side of the head just as he pulled the trigger. I looked towards the alter. The bullet missed, hitting the cross just above Emma's head. For a horrifying moment I thought it had hit the Talisman, but then Emma moved her hand and I saw she still had it.

Farber lay on the floor, unmoving. I ran to Emma. She stretched her arm high above her head but was still a foot from the hole.

"Help me," she said, when I got near.

I grabbed her around the thighs and lifted, my face level with the bloodstain on her jacket. It was getting bigger. I looked up. Her hand was nearly level with the hole. She pushed the Talisman up with her fingers and slid it into the receptacle. A sharp click told me it had slipped into place.

Gently, I lowered Emma to the floor and sat with her head in my lap.

"Is it done?" she asked.

"Yes," I told her.

She nodded and smiled.

I opened her blouse. There was a hole in her side. Blood pulsed out of it, pooling on the floor. I pulled her handkerchief from my pocket and pressed it to the wound, blinking back tears.

"We've got to get help," I said.

"It's okay," Emma said, "It's okay."

I started to pull her up, then saw Farber standing a few yards away, pointing the gun at us.

"You," he said, swaying slightly, "climb up and get the Talisman."

I sighed. He was going to kill us anyway, and he wasn't able to get the Talisman himself.

Then he pointed the gun at Emma.

"I've got one bullet left," he said. "I'll shoot her in the knee, and you can listen to her scream. Or you can do as I say."

Then a low rumble came from deep underground, and I felt the floor vibrate. Farber ignored it. I sat Emma up against the altar and moved in front of her.

"Nice try," Farber said. "Maybe I'll shoot you in the knee and make her climb up and get it. She's not dead yet. She'll be able."

The rumbling grew louder. The walls began to

shake. Now Farber looked up, alarmed.

"Make it fast," he said.

Then a crack shot across the floor, making a jagged line in the stone. Farber looked down at his feet as the split widened.

"You're not getting away with this," Farber yelled, pointing the gun at me.

The rumble became a roar as the crack yawned open. Flickering yellow light emanated from the fissure. Farber teetered on the edge, then fell, his scream drowned by the raging flames that danced several feet into the air.

Emma stirred. "What's happening?"

Through the roar, I heard singing. No words, just a joyful sound, rising from below. All the dread and anger and sorrow inside me evaporated and my heart swelled so that I wanted to laugh even as I cried.

"I feel … happy," Emma said, blinking against the light.

Smoke rose from the flames, and tendrils floated towards the ceiling, like strands of mist. Tens of them, then hundreds, then thousands. The sight of them filled me with hope and courage.

"It's the spirits of Arthur's knights," I said, nearly laughing, "keeping their promise."

Emma's eyes brightened and she took a few shallow breaths. "What promise?"

"To defend the Land. That's what this temple is for, to hold them until they were called. But they needed the Talisman to be able to answer the call."

Emma laid a limp hand on my arm. "We did it, didn't we?"

I looked at her; her cheek was cut and bleeding, her skin a pasty white, and her breath coming in short, sharp gasps, yet I felt joy, a joy that was nearly all encompassing. Nearly. Wrapped inside that joy was a sorrow that made my heart feel like it was splitting in two. It was the feeling I'd had when I'd looked into the Talisman as we'd sat around the dining room table in a time that seemed a thousand years ago.

"No," I said, pulling Emma to me. "You did."

Chapter 41

Mitch

We flew towards the German armada, ready to be slaughtered. The radio went silent. No one said a word. I expected they were all thinking the same thing I was: "What good are we going to do against that?"

Then I felt a strange tingling, and my cockpit seemed to fill with smoke. I panicked at first, then a calm overcame me, followed by a determination and joy, yes, joy at the coming battle, because this was what we were born to do.

The radio crackled and James's voice came through. "Gunner, did you feel that?"

"Yes," I said.

Then Chalky said, "Me too."

"And me," from Ditter.

"Cut the chatter, men," Fulbright said. Then he added, "I felt it as well. We're going to win this, boys."

It might have been my imagination but now the formation looked more formidable, like it couldn't wait to get stuck in and show the Germans they had picked the wrong fight.

"Okay, men," Fulbright said, "in we go. Hit them hard and watch for the 109s."

The German bombers loomed larger in my sight. I put my finger on the trigger. Then the radio crackled again. "109s ten o'clock high," Fulbright said. "Three thousand feet and descending."

Then Flight One's leader, Kingcombe, came on. "I see them. Here they come. Watch them Blue section."

Fulbright again. "Blue section. Break into them. Break starboard. Break for Christ's sake."

Then we were in it. I pulled away, heading for a bomber coming straight at me, the nose gunner visible in his Plexiglas bubble. Cannon fire came streaking towards me. I held course and fired, smashing the gun turret, and sending two shots into the cockpit. I pulled up and let the bomber zoom beneath me, then I dived back down, ignoring the 109's and strafing a trailing bomber as I passed through the cluster.

Then I was clear. We'd passed each other at a combined speed of almost eight hundred miles an hour. I saw our other planes were also behind the enemy, along with a few dozen more that had joined the fight. We cut tight turns and chased after them.

My heart pounded and sweat stung my eyes. I blinked it away and came up behind another bomber, moving up and down and side to side to avoid the tail gunner. I rose above it and aimed for its centre. Two Messerschmitts came towards me. I ignored them and fired on the bomber, hitting the fuselage and clipping the starboard engine, which began to smoke. I dived below the bombers to avoid the Messerschmitts and climbed again to fire from below. I hit one, then two, and then ran out of ammo.

It was time to head home. I turned away, looking for Messerschmitts. There were none. In the distance, glowing under the morning sun, I saw the coastline of Britain.

Then the Spitfire juddered as bullets slammed into the fuselage. I looked behind me. A Messerschmitt was on my tail. How did he get there? I pushed the stick forward, diving and rolling as more bullets whizzed by my port side. Holes appeared in the wing, but the little Spitfire still responded. It was a tenacious plane, a miracle machine, really. I pulled back and went into a climb, trying to loop over the Messerschmitt, but the German stayed right behind me. Ahead now were the green fields of southern England, behind was the Messerschmitt and the grey, choppy waters of the Channel.

I smelled oil and prayed the plane hadn't been damaged. I did a barrel roll and pointed the plane straight down, gaining speed, zigging and zagging, desperately trying to shake the German. But more bullets flew around me, and the plane began to sputter.

Smoke filled the cockpit. Even through my goggles it stung my eyes. I looked around. There was no one to help. In the distance, I saw the rest of the squadrons continuing their attack on the German bombers. I was alone, in a wounded Spitfire, screaming towards the icy water. I pulled back on the stick. It vibrated in my hand, and I struggled to level out.

I rolled the plane again, to the right, then left, and another round of bullets zipped past me. Smoke trailed from the engine, obscuring my view. I held the mask tight to my face to keep the smoke from choking me, and checked the instruments to be sure I was flying level. It was hard to see through the smoke, but it was clear I wasn't. I gave it more power. The vibrations of the engine reverberated through the cockpit. I pulled back on the stick, but the Spitfire continued its downward plunge. Through the smoke, I glimpsed the grey water, and my heart sank. There was no hope. The Messerschmitt had broken off, returning to the fight, already counting me as a kill.

I cut the throttle and pulled the stick. The plane moved closer to level, but it was no use trying to gain altitude. Through the haze of smoke, I saw the Channel getting closer, then flames shot from the engine, enveloping the cockpit and further obscuring my vision. Heat seeped through my sidcot suit, and the stick grew hot in my hand. It was now a toss-up if I would burn to death or drown.

But Charlie had done it. He'd set Arthur's knights free. And I knew the pilots in the other squadrons had felt the same thing we had. The Land was safe.

Off my starboard wing, I saw the Channel rushing up to meet me and realized this was what I had seen in the Talisman. It brought a feeling of calm. Somehow, I had always known it would end this way.

Chapter 42

Charlie

"C'mon, Emma, get up."

The fires had died, the spirits had been released, the chasm had closed. There was nothing in my mind now except the need to save Emma.

"Cold," she said.

I heaved her up, more carrying her than helping her walk. I draped her arm around my neck and held her around the waist, keeping pressure on the handkerchief over her wound. It was difficult walking, especially with the cloak, but I didn't want to stop to take it off.

We shuffled across the stone floor of the temple and headed back up the hallway. At the base of the stairs, I saw the sliver of daylight above, looking impossibly far away. I climbed, step by step, pulling Emma along with me. Halfway up, I was sure I would faint from exhaustion, but I couldn't allow that. I gritted my teeth and took one more step, then another. At last, I made it to the top and, together, we fell out of the crevice onto the grass.

Emma moaned.

I staggered to my feet and grabbed the stone, turning it the other way. The ground rumbled. The opening drew in on itself and disappeared. I paid no attention.

Carrying Emma down the hill was going to be impossible. Below, I saw people running from the houses, across the fields to the farm road at the base of the Tor. The people were shouting to each other, but I couldn't make out what they were saying. I waved my arms and shouted to them, but they didn't see or hear me.

I took the cloak off, laid it on the ground and rolled Emma onto it. Then I tugged it over the lip of the level ground and, together, we slid to the next cutting. I did this again, and again. At last, the people below saw me. I slid down to the next level. Several women and a few teen-aged boys climbed up to us. One of the women was in a khaki uniform.

"She's been shot," I said, before they could ask anything.

"Shot?" one of the boys asked.

"Poor lamb," the woman in the uniform said. She bent low over Emma and stretched her eye open with her thumb and index.

"Yes," I said to the boy, "shot. We were just out walking, and a man came to us and tried to rob us. Then he shot my friend."

"Where'd he go?" the boy asked his face bright with excitement.

"He's on the other side. He headed for the road."

"That his car?" another one asked.

I looked to where he was pointing. Now visible behind a stand of small trees and bushes, I saw Farber's car. He must have arrived before us, somehow climbed up the Tor and waited until we opened the temple.

"It might be," I said to him, "but he left on foot."

The boy bounded down the slope, shouting to his

companions, "Then he won't get far. Come on! We need to go after him. Kev, get your dad's truck." And then only the women were left.

Together we hauled Emma to level ground, carrying her in the cloak.

"Elsie, call the ambulance," the woman in the uniform said. "Sue, get my kit. Off you go!"

The two women ran across the field to the houses, leaving me with the woman in the uniform, who was now checking Emma's pulse while I kept pressure on her wound.

"Maisie," the woman said, I supposed, by way of introduction. "Nurse with the ATS. And lucky for you I am."

"Charlie," I said, "and Emma. And thanks. Is she going to be okay?"

"She's alive, but she's lost a lot of blood. And the wound is in an awkward place. I can't elevate it. So, keep pressure on it."

I nodded, hoping the ambulance would get there soon.

"Did this happen during the earthquake?" Maisie asked.

I looked at her. "What earthquake?"

"Why, it about knocked the dishes from the dresser. Happened just a few minutes before we saw you. You must have felt it. It came from where you were. Why do you think we were all running this way?"

I shook my head. "Sorry, I had other things on my mind."

"Yes," Maisie said, "I supposed you did. Stranger shot her? That right?"

"Yes," I said, keeping my eyes down.

238

"You know, MPs came around this morning, asking after a young man and woman. Man had a Canadian accent, they said."

My heart pounded at triple speed. "Umm."

"Seemed to me they were more interested in the young man. And if they found him alone, they might be satisfied with just that. If they find them both, well, they might not be as interested in getting this poorly young thing to a hospital as I am, you ken?"

I nodded but said nothing.

"They might come by here at any time. You need to get going before that happens."

I heard the rumble of a truck and looked up in alarm, but it was only the ambulance, a boxy vehicle, green, with a white circle and red cross on the side. It saw us and started across the field. Then Sue returned with Maisie's first aid kit.

She cut bandages and bound Emma's wound. The ambulance came to a stop a few yards away.

"We're going to get her on a stretcher and take her," Maisie said. "I'd say good-bye now. You may not have a chance later."

Maisie went to talk to the ambulance driver. I bent over Emma and whispered in her ear.

"Emma, it's going to be all right. There's an ambulance here."

Her eyes fluttered open. "Charlie?"

"Yes." I grabbed her hand. It was cold.

"Tell me," she said.

"Tell you what."

"Everything."

I struggled to hold back tears. "There's no time."

"Then tell me, who are you, really? Where did you come from?"

"I'm Charlie," I said, "Just like I told you. But before I came here, it was the fourth of July in the year twenty-twenty."

She closed her eyes. "And we won the war."

"Yes," I said.

"And the Land?" she said, her voice fading. "It's safe?"

"Thanks to you."

She let out a breath and was still. A tear fell from my eye onto her face, next to the wound on her cheek. I brushed it away and saw a sliver of stone in her cut. Carefully, I teased it out and wiped the fresh blood away with my finger. Then I looked at the sliver. It was jet black. So black it looked like a hole in the air.

"Emma!" I shook her.

She moaned. I took her hand and put the broken piece of the Talisman on her palm and closed her fingers over it.

"Emma!"

She drew a small breath. "Wha …?"

I saw Maisie and the ambulance driver coming our way, carrying a stretcher.

"Hold onto this," I said, clasping her hand. "It will keep you safe. It saved Princess Victoria; it can save you. Hold it. Don't let it go."

"Sorry, son," the ambulance driver said, laying the stretcher next to Emma, "we've got to her take now."

Sue came to help. They lifted her and laid her on the stretcher.

"Keep it," I said, "until I see you again."

Maisie jumped into the back of the ambulance and had a saline bottle ready even before Sue and the driver slid Emma inside. Sue jumped in after her. The driver slammed the door, then looked back at me. "You need a ride?"

I shook my head and pointed to Farber's car. "No. I'll follow."

They drove away, swaying on the uneven ground as they made their way towards the road. I looked around. I was alone. But turning onto the farm track was a military jeep. I stood and picked up the cloak, walking towards them. I stopped to look in Farber's car. There were no keys in it, and it was a standard transmission, so I couldn't drive it anyway. I walked on, then stopped, and waited for the jeep.

They sped towards me, stirring up dust, and skidded to a stop only a few feet away. Both the MPs jumped out. They were big men with stern faces.

"You Richard Hamlin?"

I looked up at the man. "Yes."

He swung his fist and hit me in the face. I fell to the ground. When I put my hand to my nose, it came away bloody.

"Liar!" he said. "You're a traitor. Now get up."

The two of them yanked me to my feet and cuffed my hands. They tried to make me leave the cloak behind, but I told them it was mine and I was bringing it. They decided it wasn't worth beating me up anymore, so they let me get in the jeep, holding the cloak in my arms. I sat in back, with one of the MPs next to me. The other started the jeep, took a tight turn in the field, and headed east.

Chapter 43

Mitch

The Spitfire slammed into the Channel so hard I thought it had hit land. The harness cut into me, even through my sidcot suit, as I lurched forward. The canopy shattered. A wave crashed over the burning engine, flooding the cockpit. I wrenched my helmet and goggles off, sputtering and gasping, trying to keep my head above water.

The plane was sinking. Rapidly. Seawater poured over the sides of the cockpit as the plane came to rest. I hit the harness release and reached up to unlatch the canopy. It was nearly under water and gripping it was difficult with my gloves. I strained, bracing myself against the dashboard. It slid back a foot, then two. I gulped in air as the water rushed over my head and the plane submerged.

I struggled through the opening, feeling painful pressure in my ears. The world began to darken, and I sank further. Then I pulled free, but I didn't bob to the surface like a cork. Instead, I rose slowly, afraid my lungs would burst before I reached the surface.

I kicked and tried to move my arms but the sidcot suit filled with water and its bulk made movement difficult. Pulling my gloves off, I tried to unhook the parachute with numb fingers. At last, it fell away, and I rose a little faster. When I broke the surface, I gulped in air, got a mouthful of water and sank again. I struggled upward, splashing, gasping, and spitting water. When I resurfaced, I tried to lay on my back as I'd been told to do, but water kept washing over my face. I sputtered, trying to tread water, but the sea kept dragging me down. My head went under. I kicked my legs and flailed my arms, but nothing worked. My lungs burned. My head felt light. Then someone grabbed my hand.

I reached up with my other arm and hit the side of a boat. Another hand grabbed me and pulled me up, coughing and retching. I hung that way for a few moments. The person holding me was struggling. I got my hands on the edge of the boat and heaved myself up. A hand gripped my sidcot suit by the waist and pulled and eventually I flopped into the boat on top of my saviour. I took a few breaths and wiped the water from my eyes.

"Annie?"

She nodded. "Come on. Let's get you up."

She helped me to a seat. It was a small boat with an outboard motor, a bench seat, and a pile of blankets. I gasped and felt my limbs grow weak. Now that it was over, I began to shiver violently.

"You're in shock," Annie said, "and freezing."

She pulled off the Mae West, then undid the sidcot suit and helped me out of it. Water poured onto the deck, and she moved the blankets into the bow to keep them dry.

"Your shirt and trousers, now," she said.

My fingers wouldn't work, so she undid the buttons and stripped my shirt off, pulling my undershirt over my head, and then removed my pants.

"Get in the blankets."

She had to help me off the bench. I shuffled in a crouch as she held me up, then laid me down and covered me. I shook so hard I could barely talk.

"What are you doing here?"

She laid down next to me and pulled me to her. I could feel her warmth through the blankets.

"Saving you."

"But … how …?"

She reached a hand under the blankets and felt my chest. "Your skin is ice cold."

I took several deep breaths and tried to stop shivering. Annie sat up and removed her bulky jacket and her shirt. Then she got under the blankets with me. "Calm," she said in a soothing voice. "You need to warm up."

Her warm skin pressed against mine, and my shivering began to ease. I looked into her eyes and saw the girl I had met two years, or twenty-four of her years, ago.

"The Talisman," she said. "I picked it up when it rolled across the floor after it fell from Farber's pocket. That's why I couldn't help after that. The Talisman drew me in. It showed me what I needed to know."

"You saved me," I said.

She hugged me around the neck. "Oh, my brave soldier."

She kissed me again, and I finally started to warm up.

Chapter 44

Charlie

I thought it was a joke, and couldn't help saying so.

Farrow's eyes narrowed. He remained sitting behind his desk, his arms folded in front of him.

"Do I look like I'm joking?"

"Executed? By firing squad?" I asked. "For what?"

I'd been taken to a nearby RAF base and put in a plane with the two MPs. We'd landed at another base somewhere in Sussex and the MPs drove me in a jeep back to the one eight eight Squadron. I had been allowed to shower and wash the grime and blood off me. Then they dressed me in my old cadet uniform and marched me to Farrow's office. I was surprised to see Mitch there, also dressed in his cadet uniform, flanked by a set of his own MPs. It was clear we were not there to receive a commendation, but a death sentence seemed a little extreme.

Farrow stood, leaning with his palms on the desktop. "You deserted your post in a time a war. That is an automatic death sentence." He turned his eyes towards Mitch. "And you, two missions, two planes. You are obviously here to sabotage our efforts."

"Sir," Mitch said. "I also shot down several enemy—"

"So you say."

Farrow stood straight, his hands behind his back. "What you did or didn't do, what your friend did or didn't do, that is all immaterial. You are spies, and have therefore been sentenced to death."

"Spies?" I said. "We're not—"

"Send them in," Farrow said, barking an order to the MP guarding the door.

Behind us, the door opened, and two RAF pilots walked in. They marched forward and stood at attention next to us.

"Names," Farrow ordered.

The pilots were young, both with short hair and serious faces.

"Flight Officer Jonathan Kent," the closest one to me said.

"Flight Officer Richard Hamlin," said the other.

Farrow smiled. "That will be all."

I knew the game was up. My stomach clenched and my head felt so light that I wasn't sure what I was going to do first, throw up or faint. As it was, I did neither. I wasn't going to give Farrow the satisfaction.

The pilots about faced and marched out the door. Farrow took a piece of paper off his desk. "For infiltrating an RAF Squadron, impersonating RAF Officers, and working against His Majesty's government, you have been sentenced to execution by firing squad."

I looked at Mitch. His jaw clenched as he struggled to remain silent. I felt the same. It was grossly unjust, but nothing was going to change that. I expected we'd be shot at dawn, which would mean a long and gruelling night in the cells. I almost wished they'd do it now just to get it over with. Then I learned to be more careful about what I wished for.

"Tradition holds that you should be shot at dawn," Farrow said, looking up from the paper, "but the squadron may be scrambled by then, and I wish to make an example of you. So, the execution will take place at sundown."

I glanced out the window, at the long shadows stretching across the grass, and my stomach dropped.

Farrow laid the paper back on his desk, squaring it up in the centre. "Everything has been approved. I shall make arrangements immediately, and you will be handed over to Colonel Merrick. Some in HQ are not pleased with this decision and he is here to make certain it is done correctly."

Somehow, that didn't make me feel any better.

Farrow came around his desk. "Colonel Merrick is waiting for you in the inner office." To the MPs he said, "Take them to him. Then report to me at the execution site."

Farrow walked past us. The MPs ushered us forward, to a door in the back wall. One of them opened it. We stepped through and the door closed behind us.

The inner office was more like an old-fashioned drawing room in a mansion. Dark panelling covered the walls. There was a small bar on one side with bottles and fancy glasses, and a table and chairs near a window with a box of cigars and an ash tray on it. At the back of the room was a large, framed painting of a Spitfire. An officer in a khaki uniform and cap stood facing it, his hands behind his back.

We walked to the centre of the room and waited. The officer continued to admire the painting, rocking slightly on his heels.

"Wing Commander Farrow is quite keen on his executions," the Colonel said. "He's still fighting the Great War, but the Army has moved on. There are many opposed to what he has planned for you."

I began to feel hope rising in my chest, then the Colonel continued.

"Unfortunately, Commander Farrow still has a few friends in high places, and I am afraid I am unable to countermand the order."

Any hope I'd felt turned to ice. Then Colonel Merrick turned around.

His grey hair was trimmed short. as was his moustache and beard, which clearly showed the scar on his cheek, shaped like a question mark, that ran up the side of his face, curved around his right eye and ended in the middle of his eyebrow.

He smiled at us. "I can, however, give you a little help."

Chapter 45

Mitch

When I saw who Colonel Merrick was, I allowed myself to feel a little hopeful.

After Annie rescued me, and we got to shore, she drove me back to the base. She kissed me when I got out of the car and promised to see me again, no matter how long it took. I entered the base, expecting to be greeted by the other pilots, but two MPs arrested me. They made me change into my old cadet uniform and marched me to Farrow's office. Soon after I got there, they brought Charlie in, and our prospects turned suddenly bleak.

But now. Colonel Merrick was going to help us, and the tightness in my chest began to ease.

"We're fortunate that Commander Farrow is giddy with the prospect of having you both shot, it has enabled me to set the stage properly."

Merrick went to a small bar, pulled a bottle out of his pocket, and poured it into two shot glasses.

"What is required for your safe return," he said, "is the proper location, the proper arrangements, and the proper timing."

He picked up the two glasses and turned to us. "Farrow, himself, insisted you be dressed in the clothes you arrived in. He didn't wish to sully an RAF uniform. As for location, it wasn't hard to convince him that the best place for your execution would be against the stone wall that survived the bombing of your erstwhile barracks. The stakes you will be tied to are very close to where you appeared, and that will suffice."

He came to us and handed us each a glass. Then he returned to the bar.

"The most important bit of the arrangement, you hold in your hand," he said, and winked.

I was pretty sure I knew what it was. He'd used it on us once before to help us escape from Reinhart and his men. I looked at the drink, then at Merrick. He nodded, so I drank it. Charlie did the same. It tasted just as vile as I remembered.

"The final piece of the puzzle is your cloak," he said, opening a cabinet beneath the bar. From within, he pulled out our cloak. "Fortunately, Charlie managed to bring this back with him, and I was able to convince Farrow to allow me to blindfold you with it."

He took the glasses back and set them on the bar.

"Now, it merely remains to get the timing right. That will require stalling for time. But I am afraid we will not be allowed to tarry here for very long."

As if on cue, the MPs knocked on the door and ordered us to come out. Merrick walked in front of us and, when the MPs tried to handcuff us, he ordered them to stop.

We all walked together, out of the office and onto the road leading back to where our barracks used to be, with Merrick leading the way, Charlie and I following, and the MPs bringing up the rear. He kept up a steady, but slow pace, and by the time we got there, I was feeling sleepy.

Farrow had ordered the whole base to turn out. They were gathered in rows, standing at parade rest, facing the stone wall where two wooden poles had been driven into the ground. About twenty feet from the stakes were seven men lined up holding rifles. Farrow stood a little way from them, at attention, looking not at all pleased.

We walked down the road and Merrick led us to the posts. The MPs tied our hands behind our backs and joined the other spectators. Behind us was the stone wall, the only wall that survived the Zeppelin attack and the Stuka bomb, and which we had appeared next to in 1916, and again just four days earlier.

Merrick stood next to us, holding the cloak, staring out at the rows of airmen, pilots, and military police.

"Do you have any last words?" he asked.

I looked at Charlie. He must have been more tired than I was, as he looked like he was ready to fall asleep. He shook his head. Merrick turned to me and nodded his head slightly and I knew it was up to me to buy a little more time. I stood as straight as I could and started talking. I didn't say much, but by the time I was done, I felt ready to drop.

"Can we get on with it," Farrow shouted.

Merrick stepped in front of us and held up the cloak. We were very close together, so the cloak easily covered both of us. Merrick took his time tucking it around our heads so it would stay put.

"Relax," he whispered, "and let the potion work."

Then he stepped away.

A few seconds later Farrow's voice rang out.

"Ready!"

Rifles clacked. Silence returned.

"Aim."

I wasn't asleep yet, and a surge of adrenaline shot through me, making me more alert. I looked down and saw the waning light reflected in the polished leather of my shoes and tried to force myself to sink into slumber.

Then a shot rang out, and everything went black.

Chapter 46

From *Tales of the Unexplained,*
Volume XIX, Number 12, 14 December 1981

It happened when I was serving with the 188 RAF Squadron near Horsham, sometime during the Battle of Britain. I was a grunt, an enlisted man, used to digging trenches and cleaning windows and picking up the mess officers left behind.

Word came that they needed "volunteers" for a firing squad. Old Follow-Me, that was what we called Wing Commander Farrow, was eager to shoot two young men—one of them an ace pilot—on some nonsensical charge. Truth was, Farrow was just itching to shoot someone, anyone, and, although I was glad it wasn't me, I didn't want to be the one to do it to anyone else.

But me, and six of my mates, were "volunteered" because everyone else, even the MPs, refused to do it. One of the boys, the pilot, was a real popular fellow. He hadn't been there long, but he'd made a name for himself as a skilled and brave pilot, and no one could understand why Farrow wanted him shot, even though, as it turned out, he wasn't really who he said he was. That made him a bit dodgy, but it didn't alter the fact that he was a good pilot.

The other fella, I'm not so sure about. He'd only been there a day and he deserted. And he wasn't who he said he was, either. I guess Farrow just wasn't as keen to get to the bottom of the mystery as he was to have someone shot, so he ordered us to execute them.

The whole base turned out. Farrow insisted. He wanted to make a lesson of the lads, and no one was very keen to learn it. But we had our orders and at least no one was standing in a line aiming rifles at us.

An army colonel was there too. A strange fella. Blindfolded them with a big, blue blanket. But before he did, he asked them to say something, so the young pilot pipes up.

"My job here is finished," he says, "but yours is just beginning. You are the knights, now. It is you who must rise to defend the Land. Their spirits have awakened. They are in you, and, with them, you cannot fail."

Everyone went silent then. The colonel tucked the heavy blanket around them and stepped away. Farrow, eager as ever, called, "Ready!"

I chambered my round and put the rifle to my shoulder.

Then Farrow shouts, "Aim!"

My plan, right from the get-go, was to aim to miss, so I sighted up the space between the two lads. It was pretty small, but I'm a good shot and I was fairly certain I could fire my round and not hit either of them. I doubted the other six on the squad would all do the same, and it wouldn't have helped if they did. Farrow would make us do it again, or he'd shoot them himself.

Anyway, I'm aiming to miss, and getting nervous, and Farrow was enjoying the moment, and doesn't my finger tug on the trigger.

I wanted to die right then. The report echoed

through the silence and Farrow glared at me. Then, when he saw what I'd done, and that I'd missed on purpose, he waved me out of line and made me stand to the side. I was sure I'd be in the brig that night.

But at that moment, he wasn't interested in busting me, he looked to the firing squad and shouted "Fire!"

Six rifles sounded. I closed my eyes, listening to the echoes fade, and noticed that everything had gone silent. So, I opened my eyes, and the lads were gone.

I don't mean dead; I mean not there. The posts they had been tied to were empty. The lads, and the blanket, had disappeared. All that remained were the ropes they had been tied with, and they were lying at the base of the posts, the knots still in them. It was as if they had simply evaporated.

Then the strangest thing happened: everyone—the pilots, the enlisted men, the MPs, even the firing squad—began to cheer.

Farrow raged and threatened until his face was red as a raspberry, but he couldn't put us all on report, so he stalked away, with the army colonel following after him.

We were all confined to barracks after that. An investigation was launched, the MPs searched and questioned and came up empty. In the morning, government men came and made us all sign the Official Secrets Act, meaning we weren't allowed to tell anyone anything about what we had seen.

After the investigation wound down, Farrow was busted to captain. Army captain. They put him in charge of a platoon and sent him to North Africa. I understand it didn't go well for him.

Even though that all happened forty-one years

ago, I could still, technically, be arrested now for telling the truth. But if they want me, they can come and get me. I know what I saw, and putting me in jail won't change what I know happened.

Epilogue
Saturday. 28 August 2021

Charlie

This time we arrived carrying the cloak. Its power dissipated, or at least asleep, it was packed in Mitch's rucksack, which he hurriedly pulled from the cab's trunk.

"Are you sure this is the right place?" Mitch asked.

The cab driver leaned out the window and shrugged. "You wanted the Old Wickhurst Lane. This is Old Wickhurst Lane."

The ride from the airport had taken us from dense city to reassuringly rural countryside, but then, abruptly, the cab driver had pulled onto the verge of an alarmingly busy four-lane highway.

I grabbed my own rucksack and swept my arm towards the traffic. "This?" I asked. "This is Old Wickhurst Lane?"

Traffic zoomed past us in both directions. The forest and fields were gone. There was no sign of the RAF base. Just a maze of intersecting roads. I stood gaping, surprised by the smell of exhaust and the heat wafting off the macadam.

The driver shook his head and pointed to a crossing a few yards ahead of us. "No, that is."

Mitch paid him, carefully counting out the

unfamiliar notes. Then the cab pulled away, leaving us, for the ninth time, alone in Horsham and with no idea of what to do next.

The lane the cab driver had pointed out was a narrow strip of tarmac barely wide enough for a car, and there was no indication that it was Wickhurst. We decided we had no option but to trust the cab driver, so we left the busy highway, hoping we were heading in the right direction.

The trip had been my idea. We had been certain our adventures were over, and that was confirmed when the next full moon after the summer solstice came and went, and no mysterious package arrived. There would be no adventure this year. But the cloak remained, stirring in us an increasingly unsettled feeling. We felt it needed to go back to its owner, but we had no idea where to take it or who to give it to. Oddly, it was Mom who provided the answer.

"You do know of one place," she'd said. "That would be a good start."

And so, we came. But before we went to the house, we needed to find The Spot—the place where we always materialized when the cloak worked its magic. It wasn't, we knew, strictly necessary, but it felt right, as if it would complete the circle. Now, however, walking down the lane and having no idea if we were in the right place, or even going the right way, it seemed embarrassingly naïve. A tangle of brush, stunted trees, and brambles hedged the narrow road, making it impossible to see what was beyond, until a gap in the greenery opened onto a short path leading to a small playground.

I stopped and gazed through the opening. "Have you ever seen so many houses?"

Mitch shook his head. A year ago—or eighty years ago—this had been a military base. Now, it was houses, brick houses, all constructed from the same, terracotta-coloured brick, as far as we could see, and they all looked the same. Each was two stories tall and topped with sharply pitched roofs with gable windows poking from the slate-grey tiles. At first, they looked like big houses, but we soon realized they were small townhouses stuck together in one block. And the blocks were set so close to one another that they might as well have been joined themselves. There was little grass to be seen, and hardly a tree or a bush in sight.

In front of us, the tiny playground—grudgingly wedged between the imposing structures—offered a smattering of childish diversions. In the centre, a single holly bush grew, protected by a circle of decorative bricks.

"That's it," Mitch said. He walked down the path and opened the gate in the waist-high, chain-link fence.

"You sure?" I asked, coming up behind him.

"It has to be."

We stood on either side of the bush, gazing down at it.

"It's like the first time we came," I said.

Mitch reached out and touched one of the spiky leaves. "Yes. What are the odds. This must be the spot."

"Shouldn't we feel something, then?"

"Like what?"

"I don't know. A tingle, or maybe we should lie down next to it and cover up with the cloak to see if it whisks us back to Wynantskill."

Mitch shook his head. "Why? So we can spend another thousand dollars and seventeen hours getting back here?"

"Well, it would be nice to have some sort of proof."

Mitch sighed. "What sort of proof do you need?"

I thought about it for a few moments, then stepped forward, as close to the holly bush as I could get, and closed my eyes.

There was no tingle, but I felt a strange sensation, a feeling of openness and the absence of people, and the air took on the musty scent of damp earth and vegetation instead of the smell of warm macadam and car exhaust. The hum of the highway dimmed, replaced by an absolute, almost unsettling, silence as the stillness of past ages embraced me.

"Oy! What are you up to?"

I opened my eyes. A woman with long black hair and numerous tattoos peeking from beneath a white, sleeveless blouse had come to a second gate leading to the houses. She eyed us suspiciously.

"Just admiring this bush," I said.

"You're not supposed to be in there without a child," she said. "And you're not to be here unless you're a resident. Do you live here?"

"No," Mitch said, "but we're not—"

"Then bugger off!"

We continued up the lane, now more certain we were in familiar territory. Occasionally, gaps in the greenery allowed us glimpses of more, identical houses, and then, quite suddenly, the road ended.

In front of us was another busy thoroughfare, but it wasn't a road. It was the entrance to a vast parking lot. To our right a cluster of men sprayed soapy water on a white station wagon under a sign that read, "Hand Car Wash." Beyond them, cars waited in line at a gas station, and in front of us, across the sea of parked cars, sat a huge glass and steel structure and a sign reading "Tesco." To our left, the busy entrance emptied onto a busier road. We both gazed around in amazement, then Mitch said what I was thinking.

"We were here in the Middle Ages, the 16th century, the 19th century and again in the 20th century, yet on every visit the land looked more or less the same. But here we are, only eighty years after our last visit, and nothing, nothing at all, looks the same. We might just as well be on Mars."

We were so confused, we weren't sure about following the highway, as it didn't seem to be going the right way. Then I spotted a paved path, and found an underpass leading into Broadbridge Heath, which was easily ten times the size it had been the last time we saw it.

Wickhurst Lane was now a busy street lined with houses instead of a dirt lane leading past fields. At the end of the road, we turned right and headed towards Horsham.

We soon found ourselves facing another highway, and this one had no tunnel to help people get to the other side. We had to dodge traffic to get to an island of calm, only to have to dodge more traffic to get off it. On the other side, the houses and unfamiliar scenery continued, but at least we saw signs confirming we were heading in the right direction.

As we neared the town, houses gave way to apartment buildings, businesses, and fast-food restaurants. We passed The King's Arms, which had been there when we had visited in 1851, and a KFC, which had not. Up ahead, we saw a built-up area we took to be West Street, and then, once again, ran into a four-lane highway.

We stood at the crossing, dumbfounded, letting others pass by, ignoring their curious looks, as we continued to stare at the scene in front of us.

"The Green Dragon's gone," I said, "it's called Lemon Grass now."

"Are you sure?"

"It's been on that corner of the crossroads since forever."

Mitch gazed around at the unfamiliar scenery. "Look over there, between those trees. I think that's the Green Dragon."

"They moved the road?"

"They must have."

We crossed the highway and found ourselves in a traffic-free area, adorned with trees, a fake brook, and even a little waterfall. The Green Dragon—and it was the Green Dragon, we recognized the building—was now called The Olive Branch, but that was the only familiar sight.

At the point where West Street began and—in the past—intersected with the road to London, was a huge, circular planter with rows of birch trees growing in it. West Street itself was no longer choked with cars or horse carts, but was paved with bricks and was—we had to admit—in the best condition we had ever seen. And it smelled better too.

Where the Black Horse Hotel used to be, however, was an Entertainment shop with a Travelodge looming over it, and on the opposite side of the street, where a blacksmith had been since the mid-1800s, was something called Wilko.

We looked to the right, where—instead of a road, or dirt track, or muddy path leading to the river—a wide, paved area now led to a bus station.

Mitch sighed. "Now what?"

I shrugged. "They can't have moved the river. It has to be in that direction."

"But it looks like they've paved over the entire village and built a city on top of it. Maybe they paved over the river too. We might never find it."

I looked up West Street. "We could try this way."

We joined the crowds on West Street, struggling to stop ourselves from gazing around in stunned amazement. Although parts of the skyline looked reassuringly familiar, at street level, nothing was the same. It was all glass and flash, giving the street a corporate feel. At the place where a store selling china used to be, was an entrance to a shopping mall, and opposite that was a tunnel leading to yet another paved area.

The tea dealer had become a travel agent, the meat store now sold cheap hair accessories, the bakers was a shoe shop and the chemists—where, upstairs, the suffragettes had had their headquarters—was a clothing store called Cotswolds. It was disorienting, and we began to doubt ourselves until, just ahead, on the corner of West and South Streets, we saw the familiar red-brick, Gothic structure of Lloyds bank.

We hurried around the corner, heading for the lane that led to the old church, and stopped. The scene before us was no less shocking than West Street, but for a different reason: it was like stepping back in time. There were signs of modernization—new buildings, renovated buildings, the Manor House was now an apartment building, the road was paved, and there were new cars parked along the sidewalks—but otherwise, it looked very much like it had in the 1800s, making us feel even more disoriented.

And it was quiet, with few people and fewer cars. We walked in the middle of the street, turning our heads to gape at the houses as we headed towards the spire of the old church, rising like a beacon above the trees.

The path we picked up in the churchyard led us to the river, its banks thick with trees now, making it all but invisible unless you were standing on top of it, which the footbridge allowed us to do. It was a new bridge, wood and steel, and stable. We stood for a few moments, watching the River Arun, which looked more like a sluggish creek than the river that had powered the town for centuries.

The path on the far side of the river was paved—a not unwelcome sign of progress—and we followed it back the way we had come, walking slower now, worried about what we might find, or what we might not find.

In our earliest visit, it had been a slave house, just one in a row of stone huts built for the slaves working the farm owned by the Roman, Fabianus. In the Middle Ages, it had been the home of Pendragon's family, and stayed in his family until the Normans drove the Saxons, including Aelric and his family, away. By the 14th century it was a ruin, and when we returned in 1851, it was little more than a hump in the ground. But by 1916, it was a house once again. Would it still be there, or had it—along with much of the town—been bulldozed and paved over?

We had to admit that seemed unlikely. The line of trees by the river gave way to fields so there was more danger of it having been turned back into grassland. Neither was the case, however. We soon spied the house among the trees, still with its flint walls and thatched roof, but with another addition, trying vainly to blend in with the older constructions. The stone wall had been repaired and the gate—a black metal frame with a wrought iron, Celtic Cross welded to it—was new. We walked down the flagstone path and Mitch knocked on the thick oak door.

My heart suddenly felt like it had stopped. I thought of the last time I'd been here, when I'd met Emma. This wasn't the first time I had thought of her. Since I'd returned, I'd thought of her often, and the way we had parted. Has she survived? If she had, did she think I had died? These questions gave me many sleepless nights, but I didn't dare hope this visit would put an end to them.

The door opened, and there was grandfather. We'd had no confirmation that this was his house, but seeing him was no surprise; where else would he have been living? And he didn't seem surprised to see us. He greeted us with hugs and held us at arm's length and told us how we'd grown and helped us take off our bulky backpacks and took us inside to meet his friends.

A man and a woman were standing in the living room as if waiting for us. They were elderly—in their mid-seventies, I judged—but appeared fit and healthy; the sort of seventy-year-olds who did yoga and treks in the Andes. The man was tall, wearing tan trousers and a blue shirt. The woman, standing close to him, was a bit shorter, with a kind face framed by grey hair that hung to her shoulders. Her eyes sparkled when she saw me, and she practically lunged forward.

"Charlie," she said, giving me a fierce hug, "Oh, Charlie! It is you!"

I untangled myself from her and looked at her face. She had a scar on her cheek and the same mischievous smile.

"Emma?"

She said nothing, but she took my hand and dropped something into it. When I looked, it was a small sliver of stone, so black it looked like a hole in the air.

"You told me to keep it until I saw you again," she said, and gave me another hug.

Then I looked at the man. He still had the beard and moustache, and it was still neatly trimmed, clearly showing the scar, in the shape of a question mark, running up his cheek, curving around his eye, and ending at the centre of his eyebrow.

He smiled at us and said, "Hell-o Mitch, Hell-o Charlie. I've been expecting you."

Historical Note

There was no 188 Squadron RAF, nor was there a military base outside of Horsham during WWII. However, the Headquarters for Bomb Disposal Units, Royal Engineers, moved to the location allocated to Squadron 188 RAF in the book, in August of 1950.

In 1951, the School of Bomb Disposal, which had been based in Chatham since 1949, moved to the site and shared it with the Headquarters. And in 1959, it was renamed the Joint Service Bomb Disposal School.

The Unit was moved out to Lodge Hill in 1966, and the Tesco supermarket and Broadbridge Heath Leisure Centre were built on the site in the 1980s.

Author's Note

Research for this volume included *Spitfire*, by John Nichol, and Geoffrey Wellum's war diary *First Light*. Descriptions of the RAF base and its operations, names of the Spitfire pilots, and even some of Mitch's adventures are drawn from Mr. Wellum's captivating account of life as a young Spitfire pilot in the Battle of Britain. I like to think he would find it a fitting tribute.

About the Author

Michael Harling is originally from upstate New York. He moved to Britain in 2002 and currently lives in Sussex.

Genealogy of
The Talisman

*Characters in **bold** play pivotal roles in the stories.*

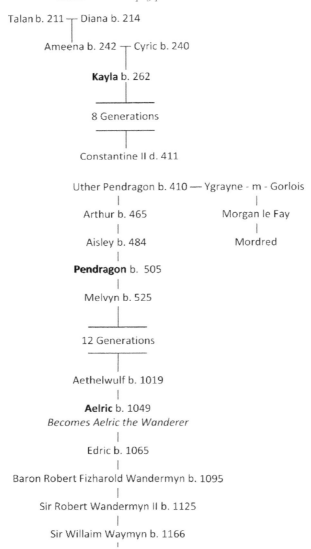

Talan b. 211 ─┬─ Diana b. 214

Ameena b. 242 ─┬─ Cyric b. 240

Kayla b. 262

8 Generations

Constantine II d. 411

Uther Pendragon b. 410 ── Ygrayne - m - Gorlois

Arthur b. 465   Morgan le Fay

Aisley b. 484   Mordred

Pendragon b. 505

Melvyn b. 525

12 Generations

Aethelwulf b. 1019

Aelric b. 1049
Becomes Aelric the Wanderer

Edric b. 1065

Baron Robert Fizharold Wandermyn b. 1095

Sir Robert Wandermyn II b. 1125

Sir Willaim Waymyn b. 1166

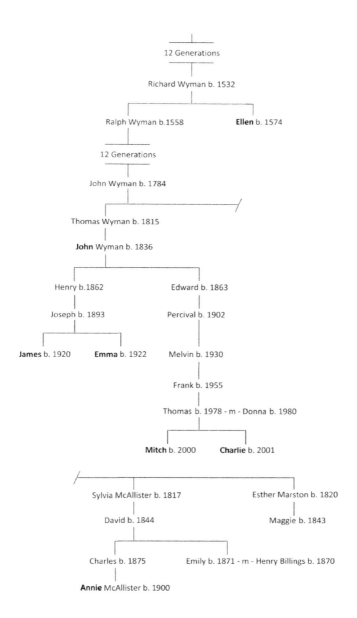

Lindenwald Press
Sussex, United Kingdom

Printed in Great Britain
by Amazon

60513539R00160